She Said She Knew What Side of the Family *That* Came From

Brian Hungerford

She Said She Knew What Side of the Family *That* Came From

Dedicated to the memory of
Harriet Emma Hopwood (Dyer),
who protected
Brian, Mick, Blue, Charlie and Antlers
through a happy and nomadic life.

She Said She Knew What Side of the Family That Came From
ISBN 978 1 76041 751 2
Copyright © Brian Hungerford 2019
Cover photograph: Brian, in uniform, on VJ Day 1945 – all his family
celebrated the victory on the Domain in Sydney

First published 2019 by
GINNINDERRA PRESS
PO Box 3461 Port Adelaide 5015
www.ginninderrapress.com.au

Contents

The Church Gate

Abbotsford, NSW, 1940

The school gate was just an ordinary wire thing. But it faced a huge church gate, on the other side of the crossing. Our gate was boring, but that gate looked like fun, if only you could get at it. The best thing was that it swung both ways. The frame was a heavy iron thing and while most of it was filled in with curly iron spikes, twisted into crosses and arrows, you got bits for hanging on.

You weren't allowed to touch it, of course. A girl in second class said that her big brother was going to take it in his billycart and put it up in his backyard for a swing where no one would see it. I think that's why they said no one was allowed to touch it. Besides, I liked it where it was.

The big trouble was that there was always a teacher at the crossing and if she saw you hanging about, you'd get shouted at and told to run off home.

It happened on Thursday. The teacher with short hair was leaving just as I arrived from cleaning the blackboard. She was a bit cross with me for being so slow, so she stood in the middle of the road until I reached the other gutter. At that very moment, she hurried off back into the school and I faced the church gate alone.

Someone had left it open and it had swung across the footpath. I pushed it shut. It was easy. So I pulled it back outside again and took a good grip. All I had to do was to pedal like you see the big kids do on their scooters. I used my right foot to pedal. It all worked and swung me halfway into the gateway. I walked the gate back and this time I pedalled harder. It went almost all the way into the churchyard.

Next time was when it happened. It was not my fault. It was just that it happened. I got the gate right back as far as it would go and gave a huge, grown-up pedal. The gate swung all the way in and banged hard on the brick gate post. It not only hit the brick post, but it bounced back and knocked me over. I landed on my bottom, but that wasn't the bit of me that hurt. It was that hairy part just above the eye. I touched it and there was blood running everywhere. My school shirt had blood spots and my fingers spread everything I touched. How could I get out of trouble over my school shirt? Besides, my right eye was clouding over with blood as it ran down my face. I held my head on my shoulder to stop my eye filling up. But it made matters worse. Blood dribbled onto my sleeve. It was too late to hope that anyone at home might be kind to me. I was in serious trouble and I had to face it. I'd try to think of something as I hurried down the lane.

Halfway down the lane, a lady who owns a girl in the big school saw me and shouted at me to stop. I did as I was told and she rushed over.

By the time she reached me, she had it all worked out. She kept saying, 'It was those boys throwing stones, wasn't it?'

She was so angry I had to say yes just to be on the safe side. She wiped a lot of blood off my face with her apron, grabbed my arm and marched me home.

My mother started shouting at everyone. I couldn't understand what she said, but I tried to support her by pretending to stagger and continued to hold my head to one side. Every so often I changed sides.

'Put your head up straight,' the lady from the lane said.

'I can't. It hurts.'

My mother and the lane lady went on about the savagery of the boys who throw stones and the lady said they should all be tied up in a concentration camp.

My mother washed my face, changed my shirt and put a big bandage around my head with a pad over the eye. I looked in the mirror. I looked remarkably bonzer. Then off we went to the chemist shop. The chemist unwound the bandage and filled the hole with stuff that stung much worse than the boys who everyone said had thrown the stones.

We went home slowly, stopping at almost every gate in Saint Alban's Street to confirm the need for stone throwers to receive the death penalty.

I was put to bed with lots of kisses.

Grandma came in, looked at the bandage and poked the hole in my face with her finger. Actually, she hurt me more than the boys who deserved the death penalty. All she said was, 'I think he'll live,' and then she added quietly to me, 'We'll probably get to the bottom of this at school tomorrow.'

The next morning, my teacher told the class all about the battle at the crossing and a couple of the big girls said they'd seen it all that it was two boys from the Catholic school up the road. The girls said they would sort them boys out, after school. Battle plans raged all day. There would be lots of ammunition and a pincer movement.

The bell rang to go home, but there, on the church-gate side of the crossing, stood Grandma, with a lady I didn't know.

I said 'Hello' to grandma, but all she did was drag me by my ear over to the church gate. She looked at all the spikes level with my face. I don't know why, but she made me stand on the bottom bit and pushed my head against the gate. She found the right spike and wiped off a bit of dry blood with her finger.

The other lady, who I didn't want to know, confirmed she had seen it all from inside the church. She said she saw me fall over, but by the time she'd got to the gate, I was off down the lane like a rabbit.

Grandma and I walked home slowly. We didn't talk and we went the long way round. That way, we wouldn't have to pass the lady who owned a girl in the big school.

When we got to the back gate, Grandma leaned down and quietly told me that if anything like that ever happened again, she would skin me alive.

I was certain nothing like that would ever happen again and I knew Grandma meant what she said. I'd seen what she did with rabbits.

British Victory

Abbotsford, NSW, 1942

I knew it was all over long before we started. The moment I walked into the kitchen, I saw it all. My grandmother was wearing her sensible shoes. That could only mean a long-distance visit.

Grandma wasn't all that big. When I stood tippy-toe, she wasn't that much higher than me. But she was substantial. In shape she was like three onions. The smallest one for her head, then under that, a middle-sized one and then a very, very big one for the rest of her, all the way down to her sensible shoes. And when she went out it was like a battleship leaving harbour, as she steamed through doors and gateways with her escorts, mine-sweeping and being despatched off with official instructions to get things done before she got back.

Not only had she laced on her sensible shoes, but she'd put on her best dress, taken her best handbag, twined the twin foxes about her shoulders, pinned on the hat with the ostrich feather and gathered up her string bags of wrapped parcels and a special cloth in her special oilskin bag – just in case. I had the two junket tablets before we went.

We left at the stroke of ten, to avoid the night-shift women from the chocolate and munitions factories, and out in the mainstream of Saint Alban's Street, she filled the footpath as, line astern, we advanced on the tram stop.

Trams have had many champions over the years. In my then whole lifetime of experience, I wasn't one of them. The Abbotsford trams were old, continually repainted cream and green. They smelled like a mixture of new paint and castor oil and were called toast racks. Each narrow compartment was designed to hold seven grown-ups a side, with the conductor crabbing along a running board outside. Other places had different trams with an inside corridor, glass doors and cushioned seats. But my grandmother said that our toast racks were cooler and the North Shore people, with their new money, knew what they could do with their cushioned seats. I didn't care what sort of tram it was. I got sick in all of them.

After a few years of regular tram sickness, even the sight of tram tracks would turn me queasy. I especially hated our own tram stop. You couldn't do anything. You had to stand there waiting while Grandma talked to some old man about what the King said to the Queen. I had never seen the King in Saint Alban's Street. You'd know him by his hat.

But there was one good thing about the tram stop. That place was the beginning of my religious life. I would stand there with my eyes almost shut and I said 'Dear God.' That's how you had to start. If you didn't start off like that, you didn't get anything. But that morning I quietly prayed that, so long as no one got hurt, would he please send over an enemy aeroplane to drop a bomb on the Abbotsford tram tracks. But he didn't. Everyone said He was too busy at the front. My dad was at the front. Actually, he wasn't. I went around the front and there was never anyone there. At our place, everyone came in through the back. I even went to the front of Miss Richardson's house next door. There was no one there either. I went to the front of every house in Saint Alban's Street. It was the same. If you could have found the right front, you could have got them to come home and we would have got things. My big brother wanted a bicycle. They said he had to wait till our dad came home from the front.

The tram arrived from Abbotsford Point and we climbed into our back compartment and took up our regular positions. I sat on the side of the back seat facing the front. My grandmother sat on the seat opposite with a commanding view of any action I might take. She kept her eye on me. She didn't say anything out loud, but I knew she was saying, 'Don't you dare disgrace me.'

This position did the job of giving me floods of fresh air while I was well, and plenty of room to move without spoiling the clothes of other passengers, when I wasn't. We sat on the left-hand side of the tram so that if I had to lean out, I wouldn't be decapitated by a tram coming the other way. She thought of everything, my grandmother. She was very resourceful.

I followed our usual drill. First, I counted telegraph poles. It was boring. They are all the same. Some are a bit square at the bottom. Some are painted black near the footpath. But really, they are all the same. At nineteen poles, I wasn't sure if I had to add, or take away, to get to twenty and I started to drift into something else. Grandma noticed. She didn't saying anything, but she made the big feather flick up and down. That meant I could forget the poles and start counting dogs instead. It didn't work, but it was more fun than the telegraph poles. Sometimes you only saw a bit of the dog peeping out from a gate. Or you only saw his tail. With a bit of luck, you'd see a dog fight and that'd give you three for the price of one. Best of all, every time you saw a cat, it counted for two dogs. It never worked and by the time I got to fifteen dogs, I was feeling swallowy and I had that throat-tightening proof that arithmetic was an inexact science. By the time we got to the Five Dock cinema, I had lost count of dogs and not only was my neck feeling tight, but I felt my hat was too tight – even though I wasn't wearing it.

The other compartments gradually filled up. Most of the other passengers were grandmothers and they looked the tram over before they got on. If they saw a swallowly-looking kid sitting in my seat, they would sit upwind.

At the main stop, a lady had trouble getting in. Grandma was substantial, but this lady was very, very fat. I wasn't allowed to say so, but she was. She had a bundle of newspapers, a string bag full of wrapped up parcels and a white cardboard cake box. My grandmother leaned out and took the cake box and one of the string bags. That meant the lady could get a grip on two handles and haul herself up and into the compartment. She eased herself down next to me – spreading out as she subsided onto the wooden seat. The seats were wooden slats with gaps between each slat and I had a quick look to see how much of her bottom would squeeze down through the gaps. Grandma noticed and that black look came at me. 'Don't you dare,' it said. She said she knew what side of the family *that* came from.

When the lady was really settled, my grandma handed back the cake. I wondered what sort of a cake it was. You needed a lot of coupons to get a cake. But I didn't have long to wait.

The lady looked down at me and smiled. 'It's for my son Jack. He's back from New Guinea today. It's a chocolate-heart sponge. He loves chocolate. Takes after his mum.'

All the ladies in the compartment chuckled and nodded.

'I hope he's all right,' said my grandmother.

'Well, missus,' she said, 'he's home for a while.'

And everyone nodded and agreed that being home was the main thing. Actually, they all nodded because the tram rocked backwards and forwards all the time and you couldn't help nodding.

Jack's mum looked down at me and then looked at my grandma. 'This isn't your boy?'

Grandma shook her head. 'No. He's my second daughter's second. He's with me. His father's in Malta with the navy.'

'They go all over the place. We never go anywhere, thank God. But he looks like a nice little kiddy.'

'He'll do,' said my grandma. 'They're all all right at that age.'

Jack's mum nodded and all the ladies agreed that they were all all right at that age.

I tried to join in instead of counting dogs. 'We're going to see my mum.'

'Good boy,' she answered. 'His mum's at home?' she asked my grandmother.

'Today she is. Got the day off.'

Jack's mum leaned towards Grandma – 'Factory' she almost whispered.

'Munitions.'

I knew you mustn't say anything about that out loud in case there was an enemy submarine under the tram.

Jack's mum nodded. 'My Nelly's the same. You know what they do? When a big bomb thing comes on the line, some of them girls kiss it. Funny, isn't it?'

'Yes,' said Grandma without laughing. 'It's bloody hilarious.'

Then Jack's mum fixed her eye on me again. 'Where's your mummy work?'

I knew the answer to this one. 'I don't know.' I recited.

She patted me on the knee. That's another thing about grown-ups. There you are, sitting there in your short pants, and every second lady who talks to you pats you on the knee, just to make sure you're listening. You try doing it back. Just see how far you get!

'Good boy,' she said. 'You'll make a good soldier.' Then looking at my grandma, she said I was well trained and I was well drilled.

All the ladies agreed I was well trained.

The conversation eased off then and we settled down to the sway and smell of the old tram. The old conductor man took our fares. He gave me an empty ticket butt. I started counting the numbers, but a dryness came into my mouth and I started to feel overly warm around the face.

Jack's mum looked down at me. 'He's another Jack,' she said. 'They don't travel too good. Jack used to get sick in everything that moves. Mind you, he didn't get sick on the bread cart, or the milk cart – he's good as gold with horses. But as soon as there's an engine in front, he's sick. He's been lucky up there in New Guinea. He says they're allowed to go everywhere on foot.'

My grandmother fixed her don't-you-disgrace-me look, but I began to swallow mouthfuls of something wet and sticky. I don't know where it comes from, but there's always buckets of it.

'Have you tried the junket tablets?'

Both my grandmother and I nodded in unison. We'd tried

everything. The grown-ups in my family had experimented on me with every concoction known to folk medicine and modern science. It was a major topic of conversation, over cups of tea, whenever I entered the room.

An ancient auntie once said I should be starved before every journey. She said, 'If there's nothing in him, nothing can come out.' She was diabolically wrong.

Then another auntie recommended I be filled, right up to the neck. She said anything would do. Even slices of white bread would work. If I was filled right up, then it wouldn't slurp around inside. She said it was the slurping that caused the problem. It didn't work, but it was much better than the starving method. Except for the porridge. That was lumpy both ways.

Unfortunately, I had an old uncle who knew everything. Every kid has an uncle who knows lots, but mine knew everything. They said it was because he'd been to France in the Great War. He said that travel sickness had to be cured by science and that understanding the problem was half the cure. I'm sure he was right about that bit. He said that nausea was caused by an imbalance in the inner ear. I knew about my two outside ears and I was a bit frightened of them wanting to pull out this other inner one and clean it. He said if I was to lean my head over onto my shoulder, it would imbalance the inner ear. It would also fool my brain. He said this was a certain cure, because my brain would try to make me straighten up my head so that it could imbalance the inner ear. This would mean two negatives and two negatives always give a positive. We tried it. It was a bit uncomfortable and it only lasted four stops. On top of that, it was an awful position for throwing up. For all that, there is always something good to come from it. When one lady got up to get out, she gave me a threepennny bit because she thought I had been born like that.

My uncle's main claim was that travel sickness was caused by a malfunction with the eye. He said it was caused by anything flickering past something at the back of the eye at more than the dangerous speed of fourteen miles an hour. He said all they had to do was put a blindfold on me as soon as I got on the tram and that would be the end of the trouble. They tried it.

It was the last tram home and it was raining. The tram was jam-packed and we had trouble getting on. Everyone was laughing about how even a tin of sardines had room for the oil. The trouble was my auntie got on all right, but right in the middle compartment with the glass doors. There was hardly room to stand, but a man got up and gave auntie his seat. She sat down and I sat on her lap. Everyone had their big coats on and it was hot and muggy in the compartment. The main trouble was that we sat with our backs to the driver. I was feeling swallowy even before she tied her scarf around my head. That part worked well. I couldn't see anything.

It lasted five stops. And it was the first time, in Abbotsford tram history, that people were seen jumping off the last tram home in a thunderstorm. One old lady managed to scramble up onto the handrail, even without her crutches.

My uncle said we hadn't done it properly, but they didn't try again.

Most of the cures centred on my stomach. I regularly chewed six junket tablets before a journey. Two the night before with my dinner, two before breakfast and two to suck on the way to the tram stop. They didn't work, of course, but they cured me of ever wanting to eat junket, ever again. I could throw up even at the sight of anything white and colloidal in a bowl.

At the stop before Leichhardt, a crowd climbed on and there were no seats left in our compartment.

Leichhardt always made me feel funny inside. The town hall was painted a bilious green and all the signs and street names had been painted over. This was so because if a German aeroplane came over, the pilot wouldn't know where he was. As if he'd want to land in Leichhardt. And all the tram lines criss-crossed in front of the town hall. That was when the tram shook you about and bounced you up and down as you crossed the points.

And just then, as we swung around in front of the town hall, Grandma said something to me. Because of the rattle of the tram over the points, I couldn't understand what she said. Not to hear what my grandmother said brought on a worry much stronger than any business of being tram sick.

I jumped over to her. 'What did you say, Grandma?'

She started to answer, but stopped.

I stood in front of her, clutching her string bags, waiting for her to tell me again. But she didn't. A storm cloud came up around her as if I had done something really wrong.

'What's up, Grandma?'

Again she didn't answer. I felt my pants to make sure everything was buttoned up. Everything was all right.

'What's up Grandma?' I asked her again.

She still didn't answer and I looked at her, hard in the face. Then I realised she was looking just past me to where I had been sitting. I turned and looked. I couldn't believe it. Our whole strategy was gone. Our reason for getting the tram two stops early was all for nothing.

What had happened was that, while I was out of my seat, an ordinary man in ordinary clothes had moved from the other side and slid himself into my seat. I stared at the man with horror. Our plan of fresh air that was good for me, of my being able to lean out, depended on that seat.

I stared at the man. I wanted to say something, but he was a grown-up. All the ladies pretended to be looking straight ahead. But they sat like they were expecting something would happen.

'That's the boy's seat,' said my grandmother.

'It was,' said the man. 'But he left it.' The man looked out at the shops as we rattled past.

'That's the boy's seat,' repeated my grandmother firmly. 'The boy needs that seat.'

'Then he shouldn't have left it,' said the man and he started to pick his teeth with a rolled-up ticket.

I knew no one could do that in front of my grandmother and survive.

My grandmother glared around the compartment as if checking on her strength. All of the seats were taken by ladies with shopping bags on their laps. They all tried to keep looking straight ahead. Jack's mum offered to squeeze up so I could sit on the other side of her.

But Grandma grabbed me by the shoulder and pulled me over to her. 'Thank you, but the boy is with me. He sits next to me!'

The lady next to Grandma shuffled sideways with all her parcels and I sat down in the worst possible position. My back was to the driver; there was no fresh air. In fact, there was more castor oil and lavender than air and I began to sweat. After three swallows in quick succession, panic overwhelmed me. The smell of clean clothes with lavender and musk suffused me. The overpowering smell of oil and tram paint made me feel I was wearing a collar two sizes too small, even though it wasn't buttoned up.

But the man sat there victorious. Ignoring angry sideways looks from all the women. My grandmother seemed to pour anger on his three-piece suit, and she muttered something about 'civies'. But she sat solid. I was certain she would have caused trouble and I was almost relieved. Besides, it was too late. Each time we lurched across the points, my grandmother and the other woman squashed me between them like two giant cushions. I began to swallow all the time.

The point of no return arrived and I elbowed my grandmother to let her know I was already after having hope. Actually, your elbow went in a fair way before you came to anything.

Grandma knows all my secret signs and she knew my desperation. But that day, she didn't seem to understand at all. She only concentrated on the man who had captured my seat. She sat immovable. There are times in life when you are utterly ignored for no apparent reason. There are times in life when you desperately need a friend, you need help – and you have a friend who just ignores you, doesn't know you. Doesn't even seem to care.

The tram lurched and my throat filled. I managed to swallow. But I knew it wouldn't stay. They say you get three chances in life. Perhaps they're right, but you only get two swallows in an Abbotsford tram. The world started to spin. My eyes went wet and my throat swelled against me. The heaving, straining pain in my stomach was out of control.

'Grandma!' I gulped.

But she sat as though I belonged to someone else. I swallowed once more and put my hand over my clamped-shut mouth. The lady next to me tried to shuffle farther away and the lady opposite started to open her umbrella.

There I was, starting to dog paddle in the suffusion of lavender and castor oil. I was going down for the third time and I sent out a plea for help. I frantically looked around. The far door was impossible. There was no option. I made a dive past my grandmother for the doorway.

I didn't make it.

As I lurched past her, I saw the parcels in my grandmother's lap shoot onto the then empty seat beside her. I wasn't expecting the grab on the back of my neck. It was painful and for a moment I thought that her fingers might meet in the middle of my neck. But I didn't have time to think. Her other hand jerked my fingers from my mouth, twisting my arm into a half-Nelson behind my back. It hurt. I felt hatred in the grip and I wriggled to be free. It was hopeless. It was too late to go anywhere and there I was, stuck, right in front of the man who had stolen my seat.

I won't go into the details, but he got the junket tablets. And he got the lumpy porridge with the sausages and home-made tomato sauce – my grandmother made beaut tomato sauce – and there was mashed potato with little bits of onion chopped up into it. He got the dry aspirin powers, last night's fried tomato and three slices of toast with apricot jam, and a mug of hot Milo. Actually, the Milo had gone sour, but it was still warm. There was chewing gum I shouldn't have swallowed, a teaspoon of cod liver oil in orange juice from three days ago and cups of tea.

He got the lot.

At first he just roared and bucked about trying to move sideways. But Jack's mum didn't see anything. Her only move was to cover Jack's cake with her newspaper.

The man screamed about stopping me. He tried to push his way backwards through the seat. It didn't work. Those seats weren't very comfortable, but they were very strong. He kept shouting, but I couldn't hear his words.

After a while, the volcano eased off and he got himself onto his feet and tried to push me away. He tried hard, but he couldn't beat the grip of my grandmother. I was frightened her fingers and thumb was going to pull my head right off. I knew she was strong enough.

I heaved again, but there wasn't much left and all I could manage was to fill his trouser cuffs and shoes. At that point, he surrendered and clambered down onto the conductor's running board outside and hung there shouting and shaking his fist at my grandmother. She took no notice. She had already won.

When the tram stopped, he got down and walked, arms and legs stiff like a scarecrow, to the footpath, dripping carrots all the way. I don't know where the carrots came from. We hadn't had carrots for a long time. It wasn't that time of the year. He just stood there with his arms out. Some of the ladies waved goodbye and wished him a happy day. He didn't wave back.

I stopped being sick then and stood quivering and empty. My grandmother carefully cleaned my special seat with the cloth she'd brought – just in case – and wiped my face with her handkerchief. She even wiped the perspiration from my forehead. I sat back in my proper seat after that and Grandma looked at me, almost as if she liked me.

The lady opposite leaned toward me. 'He'll feel much better now,' she said.

Jack's mum patted me on the knee and told me again I'd be a good soldier. She offered me a Minty. I was too shaky to manage, so she unravelled it for me and popped it into my mouth. As she did so, she winked and told my grandmother that she thought the war had taken a new turn and things would soon be better. The other ladies all agreed. They all nodded.

Just before the university, Jack's mum shuffled about to get off. As she stood waiting for the tram to stop, Grandma held the cake for her and she leaned down to me.

'You'll look after your granny, won't you?' I nodded. 'Good boy,' she said. 'You'll make a good soldier.' And, as she got down onto the running board, she winked at me and quietly pushed something into my hand.

Grandma didn't see. She was busy handing back Jack's cake.

The tram started and all the ladies waved goodbye and hoped Jack enjoyed his cake. They'd all become good friends.

I kept my fist clamped shut until we were well under way. Then I looked. It was a coin. It was still warm from her hand and when I looked, it was big and shiny-new. I had seen lots of them, but I had never had one. It was my first one ever. A whole two-shilling piece – twenty-four ice creams. The old King's face with his little beard smiled up at me from a coin as big as a medal – to celebrate our first British victory.

There's Value in Darts

Sydney 1943

Grandma was good at darts. Everyone said it was because of her heavy brass set. She was straight and when she threw, she really threw. She didn't just float the dart to flop onto the board and hang there. She used power and the dart sometimes went through the target to stick into the cork behind. Some players had trouble pulling her darts out.

I never saw much value in darts, but I was wrong. On that day, I was home from school, getting over the measles. Mum was working and my dad was still at the front.

Me and my grandma were drinking a cup of tea when the man came through the back gate. Grandma watched him all the way from the gate down the long, long path to the back door. He took a long time because he was carrying a heavy fruit box. I could see Grandma didn't like the look of him. It was probably his bright red shirt.

'Yes, Mr Garibaldi?' she asked.

I was always surprised how she knew everyone's name.

'I'm not any Garibaldi,' the man said. 'I just want to show you a bargain.'

'I'm always interested in bargains. Show me.'

The man put the box down on the step and lifted off a loose board. I could see it was full of yellow oranges.

'They're cheap. No coupons and no problems. Ten bob a box.' He took an orange from the box and handed it to her.

She rolled it about in her hand squeezed it and sniffed it. 'Seems all right, but too dear.'

'Well, what do you reckon?'

'Seven and six. Eight bob tops.'

'You're a hard woman,' he said, 'but times are hard and I can't say no.'

'Put the box on the table,' she said and hurried into the kitchen to get her purse from the top of the ice chest. She counted the money into his hand and he left, hurrying up the back path.

'He's a bit too quick in retreat,' she said and told me to get the tomahawk from under the sink.

I got it and she started to lever the boards from the top. The oranges were bright yellow and she steadied them on the table. She looked happy and I knew I would get one soon.

But the second layer was not the same. The top side was nice and yellow, but underneath they were green with mildew where they'd been lying on the ground. They were rotten. The next layer was worse.

'I should have guessed,' she said.

I wanted to tell her about putting the rotten ones in the bin, but she rushed into her bedroom and came out wearing her big hat and struggling into her grey coat. 'Come on, Mick,' she said, and we went.

We hurried up the lane towards the Catholic church. Just off the lane, there was a little home-made truck, full of orange boxes on the tray. Just as we got there, the man in the red shirt was coming out of a house.

'Hello,' he said. 'Off shopping?'

'No. I was looking for you.'

'How's that then?'

'I'd like another box of them oranges. There's no hurry. I'll be about half an hour before I get back. Got to see a man about a dog.' I wondered about a man who had a dog. Everyone had a dog.

'Bring them in and I'll be waiting for you,' she promised.

He gave a big grin. 'Always happy to please a good customer,' he said and he hurried off to the next house along.

We hurried home. We didn't stop and see any man about a dog. All the way I wondered if the man with a dog would actually give me a dog all for myself.

As soon as we got home, the hat and coat flew off onto the table. Next went on the apron.

She held out the bottom of the apron and started work. 'Mick, just sort out the worst ones,' she said. 'Put them in here.'

Most of the bottom ones were rotten and some sent up little puffs of green dust when I touched them. I wanted to wipe my fingers on my shirt, but couldn't, not while Grandma was watching.

By the time she had a full apron, the man had started down the path with his heavy box. As soon as he reached the back step, Grandma ordered me to open the door.

The man smiled. 'Seven shillings to you,' he said and tried to carry the box inside. That's when he saw the upraised orange.

'And here's a cheap one for you,' she said and hurled the orange.

It splattered yellow and green across the front of his bright red shirt. The man swore and started to turn and jog up the path. Grandma was only a few strides behind him all the way. I bounded along beside the pair of them. Every orange slammed into his back. The only miss was when he stumbled and the orange aimed at the back of his neck burst in his hair. But the next one smashed into the back of his neck and I saw most of it run down inside his shirt. Most of his shirt was no longer red.

By the time we made the gate, we were running low on ammunition. But the man was shouting and swearing. At the gate, he threw away the box to open the gate, jumped out into the street and ran for his truck.

Ladies down the street must have heard the carry-on and came out to watch and to clap. At his truck, the man shook himself like a dog and a cloud of mildew swirled around him. He gingerly climbed into the seat and drove off.

Grandma and I picked up the new box and carried it inside. We sorted out the good ones from the top layer. I thought she would be angry, but she wasn't. She chuckled all the time and muttered about how she got her money's worth.

That event gave me a new appreciation of practising darts. But you need good, solid, heavy ones. And you need to throw straight and with a lot of power.

Grandma Loved Churchill

Abbotsford, 1943

The temporary coal man was stepping backwards like he was a bit frightened. I think that would have been natural. He would have been more than a bit nervous at the sight of Grandma bursting at him through the gateway.

Grandma had always got on well with Mr Trevathian, our usual coal man. But he'd gone off on some sort of holiday. My auntie said his niece and her husband ran a little farm making lucerne hay. The husband was fighting in New Guinea and harvest time was bit too much for the niece. So Mr Trevathian had gone down for a couple of weeks to drive the horses in the reaper and binder and to stack the stooks of hay.

Grandma liked to talk horses with him on his rounds and, if he was early, she'd have me mind Churchill with his dray load while she gave Mr Trevathian a cup of tea just inside the back door. She had a special seat for him with a cover over it so that she could shake out the coal dust after he'd left.

His big horse, Churchill, was a Shire. Grandma said he stood eighteen hands. I know that was how she measured horses. He was all black except for his four, big-white-feathery feet and a big splash of white all the way down his nose. I never had any trouble minding Churchill. I just held the reins up near his face and I'd talk to him. If I didn't talk to him, he would fidget.

Mr Trevathian would only be gone a few minutes and he'd hurry back with the empty coal bag in one hand a carrot for Churchill in the other.

The fill-in coal man was different. Grandma just didn't like him. He never got a cup of tea and he was always late. The main trouble was he used to swear at Churchill. Grandma didn't like that. She said Churchill did his job well and never caused trouble. Once she had seen the new man hit Churchill on the rump with the buckle end of the reins. Grandma really didn't like that. Not one little bit.

When he arrived that morning, he was shouting at Churchill. Worse still, down at Mrs Murphy's, he didn't even carry the coal down her path. He just left it outside her gate. That made Grandma very angry. Mr Murphy was at the front and Grandma said she'd rather that Mr Murphy and the coal man did a swap.

Grandma watched the delivery up Saint Albans Street. When he got near, she stepped back inside the gate and held it open. I watched her moving her mouth about – that meant she was going to say something. She wouldn't keep quiet with someone who didn't treat a working horse like Churchill with respect.

Just then, something went wrong. There was a commotion in the street and I peeked out. There was a red pedal car left on the road. It belonged to little Ron from Mrs Riley's place. He always left things lying around. Grandma said the family had more money than sense.

The new man was shouting at Churchill and Mrs Riley was on her veranda shouting at the coal man. Mrs Hill was shouting something, but I couldn't understand what she said. But I could see that Churchill would not step over the pedal car. I suppose he knew the big wheels on the dray would squash the little car flat. But the new man was shouting at Churchill – and using bad words.

Grandma was starting to make angry noises. Not loud noises, just low noises like a dog makes before he bites.

In the end, the new man saw the little car. He walked up and kicked it into the gutter and told Churchill to 'Walk on.' Churchill did.

They stopped at our gate and the man heaved the bag of coal onto the rick of his back and hurried down our path, grunting as he passed us. I watched him empty the bag into the coal bin at the back door and he hurried back.

Grandma said something like 'You better watch yourself with Churchill. He's a good horse.'

The man said that Churchill was a useless heap of tripe in a leather bag.

All Grandma said was, 'You should know all about that.'

The man told Churchill to 'Walk on.' But Churchill didn't. He just stood there waiting for his carrot.

The man twirled the reins around and smacked Churchill on his big white nose.

Grandma said 'Caesar's ghost!' and started out the gate.

I tried to get there first, get past her. But we jammed in the gateway. I wriggled free and that sort of pushed Grandma off balance. She grabbed at a paling on the fence for support. It was loose, but she kept going. It was an old fence – Grandma said it came with Captain Cook – and the paling came free in her hand. She said it was her idea to nail it back on.

The man saw her coming. Saw the fury on her face and the upraised paling in her two hands. 'Don't you come at hitting me with that, missus,' he said. He was already stepping backwards, but he couldn't because Churchill was in the way.

Grandma was shouting that 'No one hits Mr Trevathian's Churchill,' and 'See how you like it.'

He didn't like it. Grandma hit him with the paling, not hard – well, not very hard. Just hard enough to knock him over. Well, Grandma said he'd slipped on the gravel. Certainly he slipped down under Churchill and tried to wriggle under and out the other side. But he couldn't because Churchill walked on just one step and carefully stood on the man's leg. Churchill didn't use all his weight, but every time the man wriggled, Churchill put on a bit more weight. The man was shouting something about getting the police, but I couldn't hear him over the top of all the ladies in the street laughing and clapping.

Grandma just stood there. She dropped the paling and stood with her fists on her hips.

Mrs Riley, with Mrs Hill and Mrs Murphy were still cheering when Grandma stepped over and tapped Churchill on his back leg.

'Lift up,' she said. Churchill did as he was asked and Grandma held his big hoof as the man wriggled free.

The man was angry and he swore he'd get the police, and Grandma told him to see Sergeant Burke and to tell the sergeant she'd sent him herself.

The man sat on the shaft of the dray and ordered Churchill to 'Walk on.'

Churchill didn't. He just swung his big head around to look at Grandma. She stepped up to him and pulled a carrot from her apron pocket. He moved his big slobbery lips and the carrot disappeared up inside.

'Walk on!' ordered the man and Churchill obliged.

We didn't get any coal at all for the next two weeks. But after that, Mr Trevathian came back and on his first day, Mrs Riley and Mrs Murphy came over with little cakes. The four of them drank tea and gave me a cake each, and I got three carrots for Churchill. I heard them squealing and laughing when Mr Trevathian told them that the new man had got another job and he went on to tell them that the new man said he would never be back in Saint Albans Street and that he was never again going to work for a bunch of savage female Bolsheviks.

It's Him

Abbotsford, 1944

I woke up excited. I knew there was something I had to feel excited about. But I just couldn't remember what it was.

I heard my big brother fling open the wire screen door as he ran across the back veranda on his way to school. I heard my mother shout after him to be home early for lunch and to tell his teacher something I didn't understand. I heard the back gate slam shut and I was at least glad I wasn't born a big boy into all that banging and shouting. But even though you're born too small, there are things you do know. There are things you know they don't know you know.

I slipped down from the bed onto the cold lino, pulled the eiderdown onto the floor for a mat. There was one thing I really did know. I knew that if I stood very still, breathed in hard and wriggled, my pyjamas pants would drop off without me having to undo that string. I threw off the pyjama shirt, pulled on my khaki shorts and shirt from the big chair next to the bed, straightened up like a soldier and advanced on the kitchen.

I didn't make it. Between my room and the kitchen there's the big room. And when I looked up I saw that the big room was criss-crossed with red white and blue streamers. Someone had put up all the Christmas things.

My mother looked around the door, then she rushed over and knelt down in front of me. She pinched me on the face and said, 'Today's a very special day, love.'

I knew it was a special day. But what was so special? I knew it wasn't my birthday. I'd certainly remember that. 'Is it Christmas?' I asked her.

I was excited and disappointed at the same time. How could Christmas sneak on me like that without me knowing? Other people seemed to know all about things. I don't know how they knew.

My mother smiled and clapped her hands together. She was wearing her heavy apron and her hair was all tied up in a blue cloth. She knelt down and gave me a little squeeze. She smelled awful. 'No, it's not Christmas, my little love,' she said. 'Have you forgotten what today it? Have you forgotten all about him? Three years.'

It was too late, but then I remembered. 'Yes,' I said. 'My daddy is coming home today. But is it Christmas as well?' I kept looking up at all the streamers. They only put them up a few days before the day of presents at Christmas.

The red white and blue streamers made like a Union Jack up on the ceiling, and there were streamers around the pictures of Mr Churchill and Mr Curtin.

'No, it's not Christmas,' she said and she looked disappointed.

'But real daddies are nicer than Father Christmas.'

'Do they bring things?'

'Sometimes they do,' she said and I saw she was a bit more disappointed as well.

She ruffled my hair with her hand and kissed me on the nose. 'Poor little love, you've forgotten everything about him.'

I ate my breakfast, cornflake by cornflake. I filled in the time waiting for toast by reading the pictures on the label of the unusually clean tomato sauce bottle that was always there. After cornflakes, it was a glass of milk and a piece of toast cut into strips called fingers. I thought the crusty bit at each end was supposed to be the fingernail.

Everything that morning was already tidy. The house looked shiny new everywhere and the table had the special white cloth still folded up waiting for an important visitor to come through the gate. My mother had taken out the tin of floor varnish and the varnish brush. I looked at the floor. That was why she smelled awful. The smell told me she had already painted down one coat on the boards around the square of lino.

I nodded, understanding it all. That was why she had on her heavy apron. She was going to do a lot more with the varnish. In that moment, I also knew that somehow she would get me out of the house. She must have been trying to get it varnished before I woke up. Grown-ups do that sort of thing.

'I want you to run up for the milk for me,' she said. 'I won't have time to go this morning. Can you be a good boy and bring it straight home for me without spilling any?'

I said yes and I turned around on the chair so she could buckle on my soldier's sandals. Next, I stood at the door while my mother combed my hair so that I could look like a soldier. Then she kissed me on top of my head, gave me the billy and pushed me out the door. I walked all the way up the long, long path to the back gate and turned into Saint Albans Street on the way to Downer's Dairy.

Lots of ladies were sweeping their paths as I went. They waved their brooms and shouted about it being a very special day for me.

On the high side of the street, Mrs Riley was sitting in her cane chair reading out the war news in the paper. She waved to me and called out, 'Hello, love. Be a good boy for Mummy today. She's had to wait for today. Three years is a long time.'

I like Mrs Riley. You can talk to her even when you're down the other end of the street. And she'd read out the news to anyone going past.

Mrs Hill smiled and told me to hurry. Then she stopped sweeping, leaned back a bit and went stiff. All the women stopped. Even Mrs Riley stopped reading out. They all looked up the hill. I looked back as well and I saw the telegram girl rattling down the hill on her bicycle. The women stood silent, watching the girl pass as if they were afraid she might stop for one of them. When the girl turned up into Bikley Street, Mrs Smith and Mrs Riley didn't say anything, but just nodded to each other.

I turned the corner up into Bikley Street. Halfway up Bikley Street there's the lane that goes up to the dairy paddock. I climbed the steps over the slip rails and walked up the paddock to the little shed with the bails and the manger. Mr Downer was sitting inside. The top of his head pushed against the flank of the cow called Laetitia. She was the brown one. The other two stood outside chewing and waiting their turn. They were all good-friend cows, and steam was still lifting from their backs as I sat down on the spare wooden block and watched them chew.

I liked Mr Downer. Sometimes I took it in turn with the three or four cats while he squirted milk into our open mouths from the cow. I didn't like the taste much, all warm from inside the cow, but catching it was fun. Mr Downer hasn't got a top on his head. Lots of people have no hair on top, but Mr Downer doesn't have a top at all. My auntie told me that he'd been sitting there all his life milking cows with his head pushed up against the side of the cow, and one day he left it there and he hasn't been able to find which cow has still got it. The day after she told me that, I tried to see for myself. I got up against him and ran my finger along the side of the cow till I touched the side of his head. But I wasn't game to hook my finger into the top of his head. That would be rude. But that morning the old man just sat there pounding streams of milk through the pillow of froth in the bucket.

I sat down and looked at the cows. 'Special day today, Mr Downer,' I said, trying to sound grown up.

'Aye,' he said, almost to himself. 'Aye. Your dad is coming home, they say.'

He didn't say any more. That wasn't right. He usually said something like 'How's your mum getting on? Heard from your dad? How's that big brother of yours? When you gunna start school?' He never waited for an answer, but he always asked. But that day he didn't. So I got up close to him with our shoulders touching and I looked into the bucket. The milk from the cow was squirting through the froth in two holes. But there were dimples as well, little holes coming all the time. I got underneath and I looked up at his face. I saw a big tear was starting to roll down from his eye. It ran down the length of his nose and dropped off into the milk.

'You're not a happy chap today, Mr Downer?'

'No, son,' he said. 'Not today. But I'm glad your dad is coming home for you.'

Another tear dropped into the bucket and I wondered how many tears would be in the milk. But I didn't say anything.

Soon the old man spoke over his shoulder again. 'Go on up to the house,' he said. 'Go on up and see Mrs Downer. She knows about your dad. She'll have something for you. Off you go.'

I took my billy and walked up the paddock in the sunshine leaving the old man alone with the cows, quietly crying into his bucket of milk.

The back door of their glassed-in back veranda was always open and I walked in. The back veranda was where Mrs Downer always was. They had a big house, but I only knew the glassed-in veranda. There was a mess of passionfruit vine over the windows and it made the room a bit dark.

Mrs Downer was sitting in her big canvas chair. I had never seen her sitting down before. She was fat and filled the chair. I like being close to her because she smelled of cows and lavender water and musk.

At first, I thought she was asleep. She sat there with her head down. I shuffled my feet on the floor and after a moment or so, she sort of heaved inside herself, rolled her head up and turned to me.

'Hello, Mickey love,' she said very softly. 'Come over here, my little love.'

I walked over near to her.

'Come right here,' she ordered and I pushed up against her.

She reached down with her big arm and pulled me up. My feet were just off the floor and she started to squeeze me and kiss me on top of my head. At first they were just ordinary kisses, but then they were sort of angry kisses, as if I had done something wrong.

'Mr Downer sent me up. He said you know all about my daddy.'

'Yes, love. He'll be home today, thank God.'

While she was kissing me, I saw she had a telegram in her other hand. I couldn't read it, but I could see the red part at the top.

Soon she started to kiss me again like she was really angry, and she squeezed me tight. She was all soft. But under her dress she had a sort of harness, and a buckle part of it hurt my face.

'It's a special day,' I said, and that broke the spell.

She let me go and got really angry. 'He should never have gone,' she said. 'None of them should have.' She lifted me down, heaved herself upright and walked very slowly to the big churn next to the separator. She filled my billy with her dipper, wiped it dry and forced down the lid so tight that I wouldn't spill anything, even if I did windmills all the way home.

'And I've got something special for your mummy,' she said and opened the top of the green ice-chest. She took a small jar of cream from the ice and wrapped it very carefully in a paper bag. 'Look, love,' she said breathing very heavy. 'I want you to run a message. Will you run up to Mrs Thompson's house for me with a note? You won't have to cross any streets. I know your mummy won't mind.'

I said I would.

Mrs Downer took down the scribbling paper she kept on a nail next to the separator and leaned over the bench to write. She started to write very slowly and had to sit down halfway through the note. There were only a few words on the paper, but she took a long time to write them all down. Then she folded it over and pushed it into my shirt pocket. 'But whatever you do, give it to Mrs Thompson herself, won't you. Don't give it to Elsie, mind.'

I said I would and then she pushed the jar of cream into the pocket of my soldier's shorts. It was freezing cold, on my leg, from the ice. She said I wasn't to let anyone know about the cream. There were no coupons.

I walked to Mrs Thompson's place, changing the billy from hand to hand at every telephone pole. That's the rule. It's all right when you have the billy in your left hand – you can hold the cream jar off your leg and it looks all right – but when you have to hold both the billy and the cream jar on the right side, it makes you walk funny and everyone thinks you've wet your pants. But you haven't.

When I pushed in through the front door, Mrs Thompson was already working. She had a very big front room, which was filled with half-made dresses, and the floor was covered with bits of cotton, little buttons and pieces of material cut off in the making. I liked being in her big front room and sometimes she would let me make a cloth button. My mother told my auntie that years ago there was a big billiard table underneath all those piles of cloth, but it has been years since anyone found it. I knew where it was. I could always see the legs. How could my mum say that?

That morning, Mrs Thompson was sewing by hand, even though she was sitting at her sewing machine. I could hear Elsie singing in her bedroom. Mrs Thompson looked up and smiled. But I could see she was surprised to see me.

'Hello, Michael. Did your mother say you could come so early?'

'No,' I said. 'Mrs Downer sent me. I took the note from my shirt pocket and gave it to her.

I stood looking at the pieces of material all over the floor, trying to work out how to put the same colours together. I heard Mrs Thompson open the note and heard her give a little cry.

I looked at her face. She just sat there, still, like playing statues holding her breath with her eyes closed. She held the note in her lap with the sewing. First she folded it over, then folded it again, and again until in the end it was only the size of a tuppeny-ha'penny stamp. She opened it out again, but the writing was the same. I couldn't read it, but I could see it was the same.

Then she called Elsie. But she didn't use her ordinary way of calling.

Elsie came, looking worried by the new sound in her mother's voice, and she walked right into the room and stood there beside me. 'What's up, Mum?' she said.

Mrs Thompson looked down at her sewing and started to talk. 'Elsie, my love,' she said, 'there's some bad news. Little Mick, he's just brought a note from Downers. They've had a telegram.'

'Not about my John?' asked Elsie.

It was the first time I had ever heard a big girl sound frightened. She's really a lady, but my mother calls her a girl.

'Yes,' said Mrs Thompson. 'Yes. It's Jacko. He's missing.'

Elsie gave a little scream and sank down beside me on her knees so that I was almost taller than her. She started biting the back of her hand and as she bit her eyes grew more and more starey and fixed on her mum. I watched to see if she would bight a bit right off. But she didn't. Her mum sat with her sewing in her lap and started folding the note over and over again. Elsie put out her hand to her mum, but didn't wait. She lurched to her feet and tried to run to her bedroom. I followed to the door as she flopped onto the little mat beside her bed and started crying to the window. I looked to see if she was still biting her hand. She was, but not so much.

'Mickey love, come back here,' her mother called.

When I went back to the big room, Mrs Thompson was standing up and she'd dumped all her sewing, higgledy-piggledy all over the sewing machine. My mother said she was untidy.

'Go home now, Michael love,' she said. 'Tell your mummy I'll try and come down this afternoon with a cake.'

'Will I take an answer back to Mrs Downer?'

'No, love. Just go home and help your mummy. I'm going to see Mrs Downer straight away.' As I went, she put her head down and stared hard at the sewing. 'Poor John,' she said. 'Poor little Jacko.' She said it over and over.

I let myself out through the front door and walked down the main road. A tram rattled past and the old conductor hanging on at the back waved to me. I waved back, wondering if he knew that my father was coming home.

As I turned into Saint Albans Street again, all the women were out, working in their gardens.

Mrs Murphy looked up and called out for me to stop. Mrs Murphy was the fattest lady in the street, and she shook as she jostled herself into the house and came out again panting with a big lot of flowers wrapped up in a newspaper like a giant ice cream cone. She came up to the gate, pulled it open and pushed the flowers under my arm. 'There,' she said. 'They're for your mother. A special treat for today. Carry them like that, the right way up.'

Mrs Riley in her cane chair saw us and shouted across the street. 'Them flowers are lovely, Michael.

'Yes,' I shouted back.

'Your dad'll love them.'

'Yes.'

'It's a special day today, Michael. Your dad coming home.'

'Yes.'

'Three years is a long time. Don't forget to be a good boy for your mum today, Michael.'

Then she shouted a bit softer and Mrs Murphy breathed in heavy saying, 'Dear God, no.'

'Hey, Michael' called Mrs Riley so all the street could hear. 'After your dad comes home and if your mummy gets tired and she wants to lie down, how about you coming over here with me, eh? We can find something to colour in, eh?'

Mrs Murphy hid her face with her gardening gloves and told me to hurry home.

I started to shout back to Mrs Riley that my mother never got tired ever, but Mrs Smith from up the street started shouting, 'Taxi! Taxi!'

We all looked up the hill and every gate had a lady's head looking at the corner. I could see just the front of a motorcar turning the corner from the lane. Then it came round and I could see the little black and white bits painted along the side.

'Reckon it's him?' Mrs Riley shouted. But before we could answer she was almost squealing and she'd almost leaned out of her cane chair. 'There's a white hat.'

'It's him then,' shouted Mrs Hill excited. 'It's him. Go on, Michael love, run and you'll get there at the same time. Go on, love. Don't just stand there.'

Everyone started shouting at me to run. Where to? What for?

I picked up the billy and tried to run along the footpath. It was hard to run with a bunch of flowers and a little jar of freezing cream on me leg, as well as the billy of milk.

By the time I reached the gate, a man in a sailor's suit had got out of the taxi and the taxi lady had given him a big kitbag.

I stood at the gate and watched as the taxi lady got back in and drove off. The man swung the bag up onto his shoulder. He saw me at the gate and walked over. Mrs Riley was bobbing about on the edge of her seat, shouting and waving at us with her apron. Mrs Murphy was waving her gardening gloves over the gate.

The man gave a big wave back and a big grin. Then he leaned down in front of me. He had a very serious face and a very long nose. 'What's your name?' he asked me.

'My name is Michael,' I said, 'and today is a very special day because my daddy is coming home.'

The man swallowed and tried to say something. I heard the back door of our house scream open and bang back shut. I looked down the path.

There was my mother running up the long path towards us as fast as she could go. Her face was shining red like a tomato and she still had the varnish brush in her hand.

The Conversion

Candelo

We'd reached Bega on the Friday evening. Grandma took me shopping on Saturday morning and after lunch we waited in the front room of the hotel for the special car to take us on to Candelo. Grandma said it was only fourteen miles and there was no fear of me getting tram sick.

Candelo looked friendly. There was a creek, a bridge, two hotels, a row of little shops, lots of houses, a few people, and halfway up the hill we arrived at our new house.

Mr Smith was there waiting for us. He'd arrived a week before with the removalists. All our things were spread about in different rooms and the canary was trilling away on the side veranda. Mr Smith said he'd return to Sydney on Sunday.

Inside, the kitchen was the main part. The stove was alight and straight away Grandma set about cooking.

We worked all afternoon. We only stopped when Mrs Schaffer came in with a big pot of stew and a fruit cake. When she saw me, she asked all those questions like 'And what's your name, Sunny Jim?'

I told her my name was Brian and straight off Grandma explained that everyone called me Mick.

Mrs Schaffer said her two boys would take me to school on Monday and I was lucky because the new teacher, a Miss Thompson, was still young and lovely and she'd look after me. I wondered how young the new teacher was. I was five and three-quarters. She couldn't be younger than me. Perhaps she was about ten. But girls can be very bossy at ten.

I worked at home with Grandma on Sunday. Monday was

different. After breakfast, Grandma sat me down on the veranda and said there were things about Candelo I had to know, but must never talk about.

'What sort of things?'

'Well, you know your father's at the front, fighting Germans – well, some Germans. But really he isn't fighting Germans.'

'Then who is he fighting?' Suddenly I was frightened that my dad was at the front and he didn't know who he was fighting.

'Well, he's fighting a different sort of Germans. They're called Nazis'

'What do they do?'

'They cause a lot of trouble. But the thing is that nearly everyone who lives here in Candelo are ordinary Germans who are wonderful at making things and fixing things. A lot of the young men from Candelo are also at the front trying to stop the Nazi lot from trying to come here. So just remember: you don't say anything nasty about Germans, you only say nasty things about Nazis.'

I nodded a lot, hoping she thought I understood. I didn't understand. All I hoped was that I didn't have to share my classroom with a Nazi. But there were things I did need to know. I wanted to know what sort of nasty things I could say, to anyone and everyone, whenever I need to. I never found out, because just then, the two big boys arrived and off we went.

The two big boys next door were Peter and Fritz. Peter was ten, but he didn't look like he was a teacher, even though he sounded like one. He told me to walk between the two of them in case we were attacked and that every ten steps one of us would have to look behind in case there was something suspicious. Fritz was seven and he found it easier to walk sideways so he could look in more directions at once. He said he learned it from a spider in their down-the-back lavatory.

Miss Thompson wasn't young. She was a full lady with lipstick and dangly things on her ears. She was very pretty and had a proper pen to write with. She opened her big book. It was full of pages with lines down and across the pages. I didn't have to face her on my own. Outside, Peter had handed me over to another boy. His name was also Peter, Peter Schultz, and the first Peter said the new Peter was a bit older than me and he knew exactly what to do. I was glad of that.

Miss Thompson was sitting there smiling at me. We just stood there.

'He's a new boy,' said Peter Schultz.

'I can see that,' she said, 'Aren't we lucky?' And she smiled at me as if she knew me and I'd done something good.

She really was beautiful and I had to look down to make sure my shoes were still there. I couldn't say anything.

'Does our new boy have a name?' she asked.

'He's called Charlie,' said Peter and I saw her write Charlie on the edge of the big page.

'And does Charlie have another name?'

'His grandmother's called Dyer.'

'And is that your name too, Charlie?'

She was so friendly I wanted to agree with her always. I wished she'd just reach over and hug me. I nodded and blushed at the same time.

'And how old are you?'

'He's five and three-quarters.'

'Now, Charlie, when is your birthday.'

Peter nudged me in the back and I spoke. 'Twenty-eightth of September at three o'clock in the afternoon.'

She wrote down some of the numbers. 'How lovely,' she said. 'And you do have a voice. And such a lovely voice.'

That was it. I couldn't say anything after that. I had to look down to see if the floor had changed colour. I was in love with her. I never wanted to be with anyone else.

'And your religion?'

'He's Catholic.'

'Another Catholic. Peter, are you sure?'

'He's been a Catholic for a long time. Even his mum and dad are Catholics. His dad's at the war, but he's a Catholic when he's back in Australia.'

So Miss Thompson wrote down RC and said we could play outside till the bell rang.

As soon as we got outside, I found my tongue. 'My name is Mick, or Brian,' I said.

'I know, but we got a Mick and a Brian already.'

'And my dad is Church of England. What do I tell my grandma?'

'What she doesn't know, she won't worry about. And let me tell you this: you don't never let on about the Catholic business. From now on, you're Catholic and that's all there is to it.'

'Why?'

'Because if you're Church of England, Mrs Kingston comes every Wednesday and gives scripture lessons. No one comes for the Catholics. So, if you're Catholic, you can play outside with the rest of us. The others have to sit in there and talk about Saint Paul and how God knocked him off his donkey. So there you are. You got a new school, new name, new religion. How's that?'

I said it was good, but really I wasn't sure how I'd keep it all a secret from my grandma.

'And that new cat of yours, what's it called?'

'Tom, why?'

'You got him from Mrs Schaeffer, didn't you?'

'Yes.'

'Well, that makes two of you. Tom's a Catholic too. All the Schaeffer cats are Catholic.'

It was like a different sort of air came swirling all around me. I was in the presence of something I couldn't even have imagined. I looked across the playground. I'd seen it when I came. Then, it had been just a school playground. But now it was different. It was part of a new world. Candelo was going to be something I would never-ever forget.

Ginger Nuts

Candelo, 1941

Back in those days, I was glad I wasn't born a man. Grandma said that every problem, in every part of the world, was caused by men. I was born lucky, I suppose, I could have been born a man. Lots of big people were. But I wasn't. I was lucky to be born as a small boy. I was too small to have to worry about learning things like writing and numbers. I couldn't cause any trouble.

Mind you, I used to see lots of men and they didn't seem to cause any trouble. Like Billy Shick and Mr Schaffer. But most of them were old. The boys at school said old Billy Schick had always been the oldest man in the world and he was now more than forty. Grandma said all the young men in Candelo were at the front. My dad wasn't from Candelo, but he was at the front. And she'd swear and say they shouldn't be there at all, that the war was a terrible waste and was started by a handful of horrible men. I knew the names of two of them. They were always in the news on the wireless. One was called Hitler and the other was called Mussolini. And there was another one called Churchill. The one she hated most was Hitler, then came Mr Churchill and she'd laugh when she talked about Mussolini. She said Hitler had only one thing where he should have had two, whatever that meant; and Mr Churchill she called a 'great shiny bladder of lard'. I didn't know what lard was. But I was sure it was awful.

It was because of that lot that my dad was at the front and the two of us, me and Grandma, had moved from Sydney to Candelo.

Our first week in Candelo was all housework. Every day when I got home from school, I'd get a glass of milk with a honey sandwich. She'd made the soda bread herself and I liked it warm. In the second week, I got home on the Tuesday to find we had five hundred Rhode Island Red hens and three roosters in our big backyard. Old Mr Abrahams had put up the wire netting while I was at school.

That night I fed them in the old cowshed with billies of wheat and we locked them in – in case of foxes. Grandma said the wheat would do them good and the fresh eggs would be good for me.

From then on, we had lots of eggs. I had beaut breakfasts of scrambled eggs, boiled eggs, fried eggs, poached eggs, and not-so-beaut sloppy ones called coddled eggs.

Soon I was delivering eggs here and there on the way to school, and twice a week, a lady would come in a little home-made truck and take away the rest of our eggs. Grandma would wrap each one and pack them up the night before, in special butter boxes. That was when we listened to the news. She said the eggs were needed at the front. I didn't really believe that because I knew that my dad was on a big warship with lots of guns.

One day, Grandma swapped a little bag of eggs with Mrs Vigal for a bag of stuff called yeast. It smelled like spilled beer. From then on, we made our own egg bread. The first loaves were awful. After that, Grandma sorted out a lot of wheat we got for the chooks. The good stuff she kept in the kitchen and the rest went to the hens. She said they didn't mind.

After the news, she used to grind up the wheat in the meat grinder and sieve out the hard bits, and mix it with the yeast she'd been playing with, in a bit of honey and water. The first loaves didn't rise much and were hard to chew. The next lot was a bit better, but I told her I liked it chewy. After a couple of weeks, the loaves looked like real bread. Almost tasted like bread. But it was supposed to be good for me.

Sometimes our cat, Tom, would catch a rabbit and leave it on our back-doorstep, and for two days after that I would have rabbit sandwiches for school. I didn't eat them all. They tasted all right, but Tommy Vigal always got beaut apricot jam sandwiches and I could swap one rabbit sandwich for two of apricot. I liked our cat, Tom, and I loved apricot jam.

One day, Grandma made a carrot cake. She was really good at cooking. My mum said it was because Grandma had had ten children. The cake tasted good and I took two slices to school for play lunch. By cutting up the slices with the pocket knife I used for skinning the rabbits, I got lots of ordinary sandwiches. I knew I would get more cake with my milk when I got home.

The big day was when Mrs Haffenden swapped a dozen eggs for a small bag of ginger. I remember the eggs because all the shells were speckled with purple. Grandma laughed because the hens loved sitting under the mulberry tree and eating all the fallen mulberries. I didn't like the mulberries anyway and once I had to swap a whole paper bag of mulberries just to get just two green walnuts. But it was the ginger that was important; and that's how I learned about the problems with men.

I had been a good boy for a few days when Grandma said she'd do something special for me. It started with a cooking book she didn't like at all. She said it was written by a man

She settled on the pages about biscuits. Biscuits were something she said she'd never done. She looked through to find a sort of biscuit she could make without a biscuit forcer. That's how she settled on ginger nuts. We had the eggs, the home-made flour and now we'd got the ginger. The ginger was like a small sweet potato and it was my job to grate it into little bits.

Grandma measured out the flour and put in the eggs – one extra for luck. Then the ginger was mixed in. I think I grated up too much, but it all went in.

Grandma read the directions and said, 'Well, that's stupid to start with.'

The book said to roll the mixture into balls a bit smaller than golf balls. She couldn't believe the rest of the directions. The man who wrote the recipe said to leave them round and the oven would take care of the shape.

'That's completely daft.' she said. But for all that, she left them round, planted them out on the oven tray, shut the oven door and put more wood in the fire box.

It was getting dark, so we closed the blackout curtains and lit the kerosene lamp. Tom came in and curled up in front of the stove.

We waited, and while we waited, Grandma told me stories about when my mum was a little girl and about her own favourite horse and sulky.

Tom pretended to listen, but all he really wanted was to lick what might come out of the oven. Actually, there was a strong smell of ginger filling the kitchen and my eyes were starting to water and sting.

'Looks like I was a bit too generous with the ginger.' she said. She laughed and said, 'What won't fatten'll fill.'

By the time the kitchen was getting foggy from the clouds of ginger steam, Grandma acted. She opened the oven door to look. Ginger steamed out, filling the kitchen.

'I knew it!' she said. 'I knew that book was written by a man.'

The oven did not flatten the ginger nuts. They glowed, rounder, and some were bigger than before; almost half the size again of golf balls. Grandma took the kitchen towel and started to slide the tray out. It wouldn't come. It was stuck. That was another thing made by a man. The tray went in easy enough, but the heat from the oven made it bigger and it wouldn't slide. But she was strong, my grandmother, and she started to pull it out. I was sure she would pull the whole stove, and half the back wall, into the middle of the kitchen. But she didn't have to. The tray burst free with a jerk. Grandma almost fell backwards. She let go of the tray and it fell on the hearth.

The red-hot ginger nuts rolled all over the kitchen floor. Tom tried to sniff one. He sneezed. All his hair stood on end and he shot up the steps like a furry cannonball. I tried to pick one up, but they were too hot.

Grandma pointed at the door to my room and said, 'Bed!'

I wanted to tell her I'd help collect the ginger nuts, but she was looking around for something heavy, so I changed my mind. I went straight to bed.

The next morning, I had scrambled eggs for breakfast. Not that that was anything new. What was new was the big bowl on the table piled up with ginger nuts. After breakfast, I tried one. It tasted like ginger but it was too hard to bite. And it almost filled my whole mouth.

I was told to 'get that dreadful failure out of the house'. So I poured most of them into my school bag and filled my pockets.

It was about an hour's walk to school and I still had the same ginger nut in my mouth when I got there. Every time I took it out, you could see it starting to get a bit sloppy round the outside. Before the bell went, we had a real run on ginger nuts. I had enough sandwiches to last me a whole week. Everyone knew about ginger nuts, but none of them had ever seen round ones. A couple of the kids in kindy had never seen any such thing at all – in all their lifetime.

The trouble was the hardness. Miss Thompson took one and she tried to bite it, but gave up. She took it out and put it in a spare hanky. She said that as a special treat we could suck them in class, but we mustn't keep pulling them out. By playtime, my first one was getting soft and I bit it in half. It had much more ginger on the inside than the outside.

Heinrich Schaffer was still in the kinder seats. The trouble was he only had his little baby teeth. Well, most of them. He didn't have his front ones on the top and because of that he could get it in, but there wasn't room left inside his mouth to move it about. It didn't matter because his sister Shirley, she hooked it out so he could talk. Then she put it in her own mouth and sucked it for him, from playtime to lunchtime. After that it was a bit sloppy and he could manage on his own. I wished I had a big sister like Shirley Schaffer.

At lunchtime, we played big ring and used the ginger nuts as our own tore marble. Even that didn't make them softer. They didn't even chip.

By going home bell, I had got rid of them all. Everyone said they were the best thing ever. They all asked me to get my grandma to make another batch. I said I'd try, but I wasn't confident. I ate apricot sandwiches all the way home.

At home, Grandma had smashed up the few leftovers with a hammer and mixed the bits in with the chook's mash. The chooks liked the taste even though they had to keep running to the water bowl to cool down their beaks.

Tom, the cat, didn't like even the smell of them. I told Grandma the kids at school wanted more. I don't think she listened, because she said she'd think about it. I didn't tell her about using them for marbles, but she laughed when I told her about Shirley Schaffer's little brother. She said she'd think about a ginger and mulberry cake. But I think we both knew that nothing ordinary that came out of that oven could ever equal the wild excitement of the home-made ginger nuts.

I was sorry Grandma didn't try again. She shouldn't have just given up. But then, that cooking event did prove my good luck that I was born a small boy. I can't bear to think how terrible it would have been trying to live in that house if I'd been born a man. I would have gotten the blame for everything.

The Fairy Ring

Candelo, 1941

I didn't think Grandma would let me go. I hadn't said anything to her about the boys and I knew she would need me. With only the two of us, there were bags and boxes still to unpack. 'We'll have buckets of jobs at the weekend,' she'd said many, many times. But when my three new friends from school turned up with their billies and baskets, she just said it was a good idea.

I followed the three of them, chattering away as if the whole scene was familiar, as if I too had lived in the country all my life. I followed through paddocks and even pretended I wasn't afraid of the cows. I just hoped I'd know if one of them was a bull.

'How old are you, Charlie?' demanded ten-year-old Peter, when we came to their special barbed-wire fence.

'I'm six and three-quarters,' I said putting my age up a bit.

Fritz, Peter's young brother, with the red handkerchief round his neck, gave judgement. 'Until you're seven, you have to get through the wire. After seven, you can climb over the top with the rest of us. That's the rule.'

'That's the rule,' shouted Motorcar. He had to shout because he'd just driven his ute farther along the fence to a secret gate. Although he didn't really have any vehicle, he sometimes had trouble with the clutch and it took a couple of times before he could get into first gear.

Peter nodded, but he just stood there like an old man wondering about something else. He heaved a little sigh and started to roll a cigarette. He didn't have anything to do it with, so he pretended to take a tobacco tin out of his pocket, pushed open the lid with his two thumbs, pretended to pinch out the tobacco and placed it in the palm of his left hand. He then carefully closed his left hand and, with his right forefinger and thumb took a cigarette paper from the little flat packet in the lid of his tobacco tin. He stuck the cigarette paper to his bottom lip and started to rub up the tobacco. He really didn't have any of those things, but was very good at pretending. I knew I was going to practise when I was on my own.

He put the tin back in his pocket and ground up the tobacco into a little sausage, breathed on it, covered it with the cigarette paper, tipped it all into the palm of his right hand, rolled the tobacco into the paper and licked it down. Then he very carefully pocked in the ends with a match. He didn't have a real match either. Then he carefully put it between his lips and lit the end, inside his cupped hands in case the wind would blow the match out. Peter blew out a big stream of pretend smoke, wiped a thread of loose tobacco from his bottom lip and confirmed, 'That's the rule.'

It was a sensible rule and I accepted their decision. The others nodded, threw their billies and baskets over the fence and scrambled up the wires and jumped down the other side. Motorcar had to drive down a bit to where he said he had a secret gate. The other two held the strands of barbed wire open for me to ease through without jagging my new jumper. I was nervous of the barbs because Grandma had taken lots of nights knitting by the kerosene lamp to finish it off.

I was the smallest of the four and the others stood together whenever they addressed me, watching my face. It was like they were counting freckles.

'All your family got red hair like you?' asked Motorcar.

'My sister and mother have got red hair.'

'Your grandmother's got white hair, but that's because she's old.'

I smiled a bit at that. I knew that Grandma wouldn't like that much. She'd say they shouldn't rub it in. She could be pretty stern, my grandma.

'She knows a lot, your grandma. Do grown-ups in Sydney tell stories and that sort of thing?'

That was my chance to shine. So I told them all about Sydney people knowing lots of things because they have picture shows and meetings. But I was careful to add that the bush was really better because there were willow trees and creeks and mushrooms and wild animals.

The four of us walked on, keeping to the high ground. Then we turned down into a thick mist to what Peter said was the 'best mushrooming country in all Australia'.

'If the enemy comes, all the people in Candelo will be able to come out here and live on mushrooms.'

'Won't the enemy come too?'

'The enemy won't find this place,' he said. 'They'd get lost.'

The other two nodded. We formed a single file with me second last in case I got lost in the fog. Motorcar was last and you always knew where he was because of his engine. He didn't have a car, but he walked along as if he was driving. Going up or down hill, he had to change gear. To get into bottom gear, he had to double shuffle the clutch and fiddle with the timing on the steering wheel.

Apparently, the track we were on was put there by the cows going down to drink at the creek. You knew when you got to the creek because the huge willow trees along the bank loomed out of the white fog. They were thick with streamers and they had cascades of them as far up as I could see. I knew they were special – and somehow friendly.

'Can you swing on them?' I asked. It was like asking a question without thinking properly. If I'd really lived in the country, I should have known.

'This time of the year it's all right,' said Peter. 'But my dad says you have to be careful in the winter. The streamers are brittle then. If you swing out too far, they just might break and there you are, stranded out there with a broken bone. My cousin broke his arm like that.'

Motorcar pulled the handbrake on and leaned out the window. 'So did my big brother. But my brother broke his arm in two places.'

Fritz knew more and he said, 'My mother said she broke a finger once, but the fairies fixed it for her.'

Peter stopped as if to consider his words. 'We seem to have lots of fairies at our place. You believe in fairies, Charlie?'

I wasn't sure what to say. 'Sometimes I do,' I said, 'but mostly when I get a tooth out.'

'Every kid does then,' said Peter. 'But my dad says the fairies are only for girls. You got any sisters?'

'One. She lives in Sydney with my mum. She believes in everything.'

'Do you believe in Santa?'

'At Christmas I do.'

'Does your grandmother believe in Santa?'

'I think she believes in everything. She says believing is like her cardigan – more holy than religious. She believes in angels, I know that much.

The other three turned silent as we crossed over a muddy patch alongside the creek.

I was excited. In Sydney, the other boys at school had talked about their country holidays. One of the Sydney boys had lived on a farm once and talked about it every playtime. He reckoned he knew the bush like the back of his hand.

The boys in front scrambled over one more fence and helped me through. I was hardly through when Peter found the first big mushroom. It was bigger across than his hand and he settled it tenderly on the bottom of the billy.

'We ought to give the first one to the new kid,' said Motorcar as he throttled back to talk.

'He'll get plenty,' said Peter. 'I'll give him the next one. I want the big one to show Mum.'

We spread out abreast inching across the paddock. I watched them more than I looked for mushrooms. They were stooped over like old men, with their arms hanging loose and their eyes on the grass. But I did look down and that's when I saw my first mushroom. First I shouted, then I grabbed it and pulled it out of the ground. The others came over.

Peter admired it but said it should have been pinched off above ground instead of being pulled up – dirt and all. 'Pinch it off and another one will come in its place,' he said.

I was a bit crestfallen, but I did have a mushroom in my basket. I'd caught it myself. I'd have something to put in a letter to Mum. I knew my grandmother would dictate the words and most of the spelling.

I tried to phrase the sentence in my mind. 'Dear Mum, today three boys from my new school took me to catch wild mushrooms and I caught one myself. The boys are called Peter and Fritz and the other one is called Motorcar. His real name is Hermann, but no one can spell it. We also have a hen sitting on eggs. Love, Mick.'

I would have worked out another letter, but another mushroom suddenly popped into view from behind a tussock. I pulled it up trying to pinch it at the same time. The other boys looked it over.

Peter took it and peeled a piece of the white skin from the dome. 'That's how you tell. If they don't peel, they just kill you.'

His brother Fritz nodded, and said, 'After you eat a bad one, you have thirty-nine steps left. You start running and at thirty-six steps you start to stumble, at thirty-eight you stop and just on thirty-nine, you drop dead. That's it. You become as dead as a scab on an old sore.'

Motorcar did a double shuffle before he spoke. 'Or as dead as a dead flying fox hanging upside down,' he said.

'Or as dead as a doornail,' finished Peter.

I marvelled at their understanding and I wished I had something I could contribute. Not that it would have been much use, because the little group of real teachers had shuffled off again into the mist to look for more mushrooms.

Gradually we walked apart, but now and then finding mushrooms in clumps. When that happened, they were divided.

Peter supervised the division to ensure equality for all and especially for the new kid in his charge. 'My mum said to look after you because you come from Sydney and you won't know the ways of the bush. How you getting on?'

'I didn't know much this morning about mushrooms. Now I know a lot about them.'

'You'll be right. You'll just cotton on as you go,' confirmed Peter without really looking up.

Motorcar grew tired of mushrooming. He parked the car and spent a while hurling dry pats of cow manure, discus fashion, into the fog. But after a few attempts, Peter told him to get back in his cab. He did and put the engine in first and drove off to get more mushrooms.

Slowly we separated more and more across the face of a gentle hill, collecting as we went. There were plenty and I hoped Grandma knew how to cook the ones I had. Already the bottom of the basket was more than half covered and I knew that if everything else in my new life failed, I was a distinct success as a catcher of mushrooms. I'd definitely have something to talk about for a long time to come.

That's when I came to a line of mushrooms. I picked one and realised that the line went for a long way. There were mushrooms by the dozen. All standing in line like soldiers – as if they'd been put there. I knew in my bones there was something odd about it. While I had never before seen mushrooms growing, had never before that morning picked a single mushroom – or walked through a milky mist – I knew from the vast new experience of that morning alone that this curving line of mushrooms was somehow different.

I called Peter. The others followed. The four of us stood close together looking down at the line.

'It's the fairies again,' said Fritz with the edge of fear in his voice.

'It's the fairies, all right,' whispered Peter and he laid his hand reassuringly on his little brother's shoulder.

Motorcar turned off the ignition. He looked as if he wanted to get out of the car and run. 'Are there ever bad fairies?' he asked.

'Never,' said Peter. 'But if you come across one in the dark, they can give you an awful fright. That's the only danger. And horses are terrible shy of them.'

The four of us stood as if not wanting to look up into the fog, while Peter told of a horse from some other town that had bolted over a cliff and killed itself and the rider, just because a friendly fairy had suddenly stood in the road without giving a warning. 'But there's no need to worry now. They sleep at this time of the morning.'

I knew that for the first time in my life, I was in the presence of something church-like. I looked at the faces of the other boys and I was impressed by the little-old-men look of them. I hoped that after a few months in the new town, my own face might change and I'd be able to look as old as the others. But I needed to know more first.

'Where does the line of mushrooms go to?' I asked.

'Nowhere. It's a ring,' said Peter. 'Did you take any?'

'Only one,' I confessed.

'Then put that one back and we can take it last of all.'

'What will the fairies do?' I asked as I put the mushroom back. I wished I'd pinched the stalk a bit better.

'Nothing! But what we'll do just in case,' said Peter, 'is walk out the circle.'

We formed Indian file and walked around the circumference of the circle. The circle itself was about a quarter the size of a football oval and I kept my eyes peeled on the uninterrupted line of mushrooms.

'The circle is where the fairies have danced last night,' explained Peter. 'They must have camped here yesterday and last night, just as the Milky Way was getting whiter and whiter, they came here and danced around in a big circle.'

'Must have been a powerful big lot of them,' said Motorcar.

'Must have been,' said Peter. 'Sure is a big circle.' Peter went on just for my sake. 'Everywhere one of their feet touches the ground, even ever so lightly, a mushroom comes up on that exact spot by the next morning. If you look, you'll see there isn't a single mushie growing inside the circle.'

No one answered. We simply followed the line of mushies till we were back where we started. I knew we were back at the start because the one I had picked had fallen over.

'Not a good sign,' said Peter. 'We'll have to go again, but round the other way.'

'Why?' I asked.

'Have to. It's the rule,' said Peter and then we about-turned and circumnavigated the circle in the opposite direction. My teacher in Sydney had got that word from another teacher called Captain Cook.

When we got back, Peter explained that we could then step inside the circle and that, once inside, because we had been around twice, we were perfectly safe from any and every danger as long as we wanted to stay there.

Peter led the way through the small gap in the mushrooms and we moved quietly into the centre of the circle to form yet another circle of our own, facing out like the hub of a wheel connected, by strong spokes of belief, to the rim.

'We can sit down here for a while,' said Peter. 'We don't have to go any farther anyway.'

'Why not?' I asked.

'Can't you see for yourself?' said Motorcar, and there was a scratchy sound in his voice.

Peter was cross. 'Of course he can't. And you couldn't either on your first day.'

'So long ago, I've forgotten,' said Motorcar in a bit of a sulk.

'See what?' I asked again throwing all caution to the wind.

'Nothing. But we don't have to go any farther. By the time we leave here and collect all the circle, we'll have more mushies than we can carry.'

I was a bit worried about taking them all. What if the fairies wanted a few for themselves?

'No worries,' said Peter. 'After we've been around outside, once each way and then sat down in the middle like this and talked nice things about the fairies, we can take all the mushies. That's the rule.'

I had to confess. 'I didn't really believe in fairies before. I thought they were only in stories. Do they have wings and things?'

'They got little ones, but they don't use them all that much,' said Motorcar, holding his thumbs crossed for luck.

'Will I be able to tell my grandma about the ring?'

'Oh yes,' said Peter. 'The fairies won't mind. The only thing is that they don't keep secrets. Do you keep secrets?'

'Sometimes. Why?'

'Well, you shouldn't keep secrets inside a fairy ring. The secrets turn bad and stay with you. My big brother was with a boy once who used to be a friend of my uncle. One day they found a ring, just like this one. Well, when they got inside and sat down, he said he had no secrets and said he never sweared. You know what happened?'

Motorcar said he knew what happened and he made the sign of the cross.

I would have asked for more information, but Peter beat me to it.

'The kid said he didn't swear. As soon as he said that, a fairy must have heard him and he got stuck with swearing. The only things he could say was swearing.'

'What sort of swearing?'

'Bad swearing.'

'How bad?'

'Dreadful bad.'

The others sat glum in memory of their departed swearer.

Peter broke into the gloom and pretended to look at the sky. 'Tell me, Mick: do you believe in Jesus?'

'I have to, especially now that I'm Catholic. All Catholics have to believe in Jesus. I believe in Mary too and his father Joseph. I learned all that in Sydney.'

'Hm,' murmured Peter. 'You'll find things are a bit different here. Does your mum believe in Jesus?'

'I think so. She tries to go to church every morning.'

'My mum has to milk,' said Fritz with a sort of sleepy yawn.

'The trouble is,' went on Peter, 'I don't believe they had all those names. Names like Lazarus and Nicodemus and so on. We haven't got a single kid in the whole of Candelo with a name like that.'

'But Jesus was magic,' put in Motorcar. 'He could fix people up and turn water into plonk. I hate the taste of wine stuff. Does your dad drink wine or plonk in Sydney?'

'He's at the front,' I said, hoping they understood my grandmother's expression.

'My dad doesn't drink wine,' went on Motorcar. 'But he drinks beer every Saturday. The day the sergeant told us when my big brother was missing at the front, my dad drank so much beer he got all drunk. My mum and my aunties all went to church. But my dad just stayed home and got so drunk, he just cried and cried. He couldn't stop himself. That's when he said I could believe in fairies if I wanted to. He was funny that day.'

Peter cut short the story with 'But the Reverend Mrs Kingston in scripture lessons says there are no fairies or any Old Gods left. She says there's only Jesus and the angels. She says the stuff we believe in is old-fashioned.'

Motorcar came back into the talk. 'That's because she only works for Jesus. She'd have to say that, or she'd get the sack. My dad sacked a man once because my dad said the man didn't believe in work.'

There was silence for a few moments as the boys sat in thought. I could see that the mist was beginning to thin around the willow trees.

Peter leaned back on the wet grass to prop himself on his right elbow and pointed to the top of the willow beside the creek. 'Jesus never comes lower than that tree,' he said.

'Why not?' asked Motorcar.

'Everything is too busy lower than that.'

I nodded with understanding. In that moment, I wished I was ten years old. People who are ten know almost everything. At six and three-quarters, you have to listen all the time.

'That's why they put that big pointed chimney on top of lots of churches. Jesus can get all the money from the plate – the higher the steeple, the easier for Him.'

'It's the same in the Methos,' said Motorcar. 'When all the money is in the plate, the minister puts it in a tube at the back of the church and it all goes straight up to Jesus through the steeple.

'Do other gods ever get the money instead of Jesus? Or does he get it all?' asked Fritz. He was chewing a piece of grass. He looked good doing that and I tried to get a bit the same.

Peter went on and explained that the other gods lived much higher than Jesus and they rode about in High Heaven, over the top of the Milky Way in big sulkies that were pulled by eight horses, four abreast. 'They get the horses by crossing half-draught mares with racehorse stallions. That way you get lots of speed and good bone. My dad says it's the bone that counts in a good horse. That's what you want, plenty of good bone.'

We went silent again.

I was thinking about the Old Gods even higher up than Jesus. 'Are they friendly to country people?' I asked, wondering why on earth my grandmother had never warned me about such things.

'Sure. They wave to you sometimes, if you're standing in just the right way.'

'Can you see them? How do you stand in just the right way?' I asked. This was epiphany.

Peter stood up and gave a demonstration of how you had to stand with both feet apart and with the left hand holding the heart still, and the right hand held down stiff at attention. 'Sort of like a good soldier,' he said. 'If you do that and you stand rock-still, you can sometimes see them going along the top of the Milky Way. Of course it has to be at night. You can't see them in the daytime. They sleep then. You see, when it's daytime down here, it's night time up there, and the same the other way round. When it's dark down here, they start from the bottom of Australia near the Southern Cross. Then they go over past the Saucepan and then they keep going past all Australia even, and they end up somewhere near Ireland, on the other side of the world.'

'They don't go to England?'

'No. The people in England only believe in Jesus. They're poor like that.'

'They believe in Mr Churchill,' said Motorcar.

We fell silent again.

I just shook my head. 'I just didn't know any of this stuff,' I said. I was happy. It was such a relief to confess that I had been ignorant. Suddenly I knew the world was huge. I was glad my grandmother had let me come. I looked down at the basket now almost half-full and I hoped she would be so happy, she might make me toffees for being good.

'Will you bring some to school?' asked Motorcar.

'Come to my place on the way, on Monday and if there's any left, she'll give you a little bag full. She makes beaut boiled lollies.'

'Does she believe in Jesus, or the Old Gods?'

'I'm not sure. She says she's on the side of the Irish.'

'Then she's a real believer. That's good. That means we've got everyone in Candelo believing. We won't have trouble at night.'

'Do other places have trouble?'

'Some do. There was one man in the next town who didn't believe. He went out to get an armful of wood from the heap one night. It's a long time ago now but, well, when he got there, he looked up and saw Them cantering past overhead. But he didn't believe and so no one ever saw him again. He just evaporated up into the Milky Way. The next day, they found his boots in the next paddock. They must have fallen off as he evaporated halfway up. They reckon lots of people have gone that way.'

'It's best to believe,' said Motorcar, and we all nodded.

I lay back on the grass listening to the older boys and especially to Peter. I felt safe. Not only had I found a Fairy Ring, but I had also found an older friend who was obviously patient, and full of real information. I heard myself sigh as I had noticed Grandma sigh sometimes.

Motorcar grew tired of talking and started hurling cow pats again. Fritz joined him in a distance competition and after a few shots Peter had a turn and won easily.

'He's the best pitcher at school,' said Fritz. 'He was the best pitcher even when he was only nine.'

Peter shrugged off the compliment and led his disciples back from the ring through the gap. Then we picked the whole circle. There were hundreds in the ring and by the time we had collected them all, the mist had cleared and all our baskets and billies were overflowing. Motorcar had trouble juggling his basket and adjusting the timing and throttle.

When we arrived back at my place, Grandma was about to stop for a cup of tea. She'd also made a batch of rock cakes and we sat at the newly scrubbed table drinking milk and eating cakes.

Motorcar had parked his vehicle outside and he ran his hand over the scrubbed wood. 'I can see you're pretty good at housework, Mrs Dyer. You sure did a good job on this table.'

She smiled and thanked him. I could tell she'd write it down in a letter to my mum. I was happy to see her smile and I knew she wouldn't be cross all day, unless I did something really bad.

The others hung about looking at the hens and everything till they were sent off with a small bag of rock cakes for the other members in their families.

I worked inside most of the day. There was plenty to do – doorknobs and taps to Brasso, paper to put on shelves, empty glass jars to unpack and stack away. Hundreds of grown-up things. All afternoon we were at it.

Sharp at four o'clock (that's the rule), I inspected the broody hen sitting on the eggs and I threw her a mug of wheat. I wondered just then if the hens knew about fairies and the Old Gods. Or did they have ones of their own that humans couldn't see?

That night at dinner time we sat down to a rabbit and mushroom pie. It was great and I saw a stack of little pies ready for school lunches.

I sat there chewing and thinking of all the things I had learned. Grandma chatted about the broody hen and how she expected twelve little chickens. Then she told me the same stories of her own girlhood in another country, where her own grandmother had taught her how to look after hens and chickens.

I tried to picture her as a girl with her grey hair plaited into a bun, her fat body in a long grey dress and her sensible shoes as she bounced across the paddocks with her friends collecting mushrooms.

'Did you ever find a Fairy Ring when you were a little girl?'

'No, but I know there are such things.'

'We found one today. Do you have to keep it a secret if you find it?'

'No, but you mustn't tell where it was. Which one of you found it?'

'I did.'

'Then that means you'll be lucky in this town and you'll learn lots of things about the country.' She had that twinkle in her eyes she gets when she's happy.

'I learned lots of things today, Grandma.'

'No wonder you look so tired,' she said smiling, and we sat there talking over the table till it was time to light the lamp for the washing up.

Grandma started filling the washing-up bowl from the fountain on the stove, and on the spur of the moment I offered to get another armload of wood from the heap.

It was dark, and I walked across the veranda and down the three steps onto the path to the wood heap. The gravel under my sandals crunched in the closeness of the dark. I was a bit surprised by the dark and I felt that shiver spread down inside the back of my shirt. I hoped I wouldn't see a fairy who might appear without warning. I'd like to see one – especially one with wings, but I wanted a warning first. Otherwise I might bolt over a cliff like the horse.

At the wood heap, my eyes slowly adjusted to the dark and I could make out the piles of logs we had split the day before. But this was my chance. I saw the bits I had to collect, but I waited. Before bending down, I braced my courage and stood up like a soldier.

I kept looking down, but I stood with my feet apart, clapped my left hand over my heart, which was thumping like a windmill, and I stiffened my right arm down my side. First I steadied my body, then told myself I was game enough and at the end, slowly raised my head to look at the stars.

The stars were scattered across the black sky like chips of ice. The coldness of them surprised me. The Milky Way was a curdle of cold stars like a giant's highway made from iceblocks. I stared south of the Southern Cross, followed the Milky Way past the Saucepan, and followed that line to the other end of the sky. I focused and strained to see through the blotches of frozen stars. One star fell sideways and another went another way. A big one moved a little and one went out. There was movement all along the Way, with bits of stars darting everywhere.

But there were no teams of quarter-draughts, no huge sulkies. I heaved a little sigh almost of relief. Now at least I knew where they went. I also knew why the Milky Way was there at all. I accepted it all and I knew deep down inside me that I didn't want to see everything in one day. It was enough just to know that I understood all these things. I was growing up.

I picked up the armload of wood to carry inside to keep the fires going in the invisible world of those who learn important things.

Dotty

Candelo, 1941

Dotty arrived early that Saturday morning. My grandma and I had just tidied up from making the bread and we were listening to the news.

It's over seventy years since Dotty and I first met. Sixty-seven have gone by since we've seen each other and we've never corresponded. But Dotty has never been a stranger. In all that time, Dotty has been a constant and comforting haunting.

'This your new girlfriend?' asked Grandma. She'd gone to the window when we heard the gate swing open and slam shut.

'Who is it, Grandma?' I left off wiping the dough board to join her at the window. 'I haven't got a girlfriend and that's Dotty. She's got the Power.'

'How's that then?'

'I don't know. Peter at school, he says she's got the Power, that's all.'

'She's got tidy hair. How old is she?'

'She's in fifth class.'

'About nine or ten.'

I would have said yes, but Dotty came to the veranda and put her basket down on the steps. She was dressed like a working man in her bib 'n' brace overalls. Her shirt was red and white checks – made from the same stuff as our kitchen tablecloth. She stood there as if she wasn't sure of something and then turned and started to walk back up the path.

'Hang about, Dotty,' called my grandma and we both went to the veranda.

'You know my name then?' she said. 'Did Charlie tell you?'

'He must have,' said Grandma.

I peeped into the basket. The bottom was covered with eggs around a jar of jam-looking stuff. I hoped it wasn't marmalade or sweet orange.

'My mother said I was just to leave it,' said Dotty.

My grandma chuckled and had Dotty go inside. 'I'll get a glass of sarsaparilla while young Charlie, though he's Mick to us, finishes the breadboard. He's been working. How old are you, Dotty?'

'I'm nine and a quarter, three years older than Charlie. But he's clever, Mrs Dyer. Is his mother clever?'

'Couldn't have been too clever,' said my grandma without laughing. Then she added, 'I suppose she was sometimes.' She mixed our drinks while she talked and I turned the board over and wiped the other side.

Dotty watched me working. 'It never ends does it, Mrs Dyer,' she said as she pulled her plaits over her head to tighten the bow. 'You start things all the time, but you never seem to finish anything. Life's too short,' she said in voice like people use in church.

'Amen to that,' said Grandma and they looked at each other as if they knew something secret between them. I wondered if that was the Power.

It was only the day before that I had really met Dotty.

My grandma and I had arrived in Candelo on a Saturday. I spent the next Saturday morning with Peter, Fritz and Motorcar catching mushrooms. On Sunday, Grandma and I worked non-stop on the house, whitewashing the fireplace in the big room upstairs and rubbing Brasso on and off every knob and tap in the house.

I didn't really meet Dotty until we did sport the next Friday. She's the captain of the under-10s and she picked me because I was a new boy.

At home, I'd cut the kindling and filled the wood box. Then we'd mixed dough in the large round white enamelled washing-up basin, rolled it out onto the board and I'd pounded and punched and made towers and dropped bombs, with my fists, till it stretched like India rubber.

Dotty watched Grandma take out the bread as she sipped her sarsaparilla. Grandma first took out the two loaves then the tray of buns and put a cake in, just so she wouldn't waste the heat. While the buns were cooling, she unpacked the eggs from Dotty's basket and put two bread rolls back for Dotty and her little brother George, who Dotty said 'breaks everything he lays his hands on'.

'Is Charlie allowed to come and see my mother's house this morning, Mrs Dyer? Or is he too busy? My mother said he'd probably be too busy.'

'Oh, he can take an hour off,' said Grandma and she ordered me to be back by lunch.

So Dotty and I went off to return the basket and I was quietly told to carry wood for Dotty's mother because her dad, like mine, was at the front. We started towards Dotty's house. But as soon as we turned the first bend and were out of sight, Dotty turned off the road and climbed over the fence corner post. Then she held the wires apart for me to wriggle through without jagging my khaki shirt. I followed as we went down toward the creek. The willows beside the creek, leading to the best mushroom-catching paddocks, hung lush.

Dotty walked around them to the mound to sit looking at the weeping streamers, like green curtains, but better. 'You've seen these before,' she said.

I nodded, trying to look like someone who'd seen everything before.

'Peter reports to me that you're a believer. Is that really true?'

'I think so,' I said. 'I've been practising at night to see the Old Gods in the Milky Way, but so far I haven't seen much. But I'm not frightened of the dark any more.'

'And that's because of Peter?'

I nodded.

Dotty said Peter had done a good job. She looked at the willow, but I couldn't stop looking at her. She was only a little bit bigger than me. But she was much browner and she had brown eyes to match her plaits. It was her eyes I noticed most. The other kids had long rounded eyes, curved along the bottom as well as the top. But Dotty's were different. They were straight across the bottom, but rounded on top like church windows.

'You're new to Candelo and you've got to learn a lot of things quick. Today I'll tell you about the Little People. You won't have seen them in Sydney. They left there long ago. They can't take all the noise. And you won't see them here yet either, not until you get the Power. And if you ever lose your faith, you won't never be able to see them ever again.'

'Will I see them today?'

'Perhaps. But I suspect not. Let's be content with just learning.' She paused, took a big breath and started to recite. 'It just so happens that our Little People live near, next to, or under willows. They cannot survive if they're distant from their beloved weeping willows. Understand?'

I nodded again.

'We get the Power from them. Understand again?'

I was sick of nodding so I asked, 'What is the Power?'

'It's the power to see. Look down into the creek there. What do you see?'

'Muddy water.'

'There's not only mud in the water. The creek has life – like the mountains and the land. There's a sort of blood in the water from the flood farther up. The land cries and bleeds – not just dirt turning the water muddy. It's their sort of blood.'

'Doesn't look very red.'

'At your stage you only see mud. But the blood of the flood land is there just the same. You'll need the Power before you see lots of things like that. Have you done running writing at school yet?'

I said yes instead of nodding.

'Well, you know what a capital letter is?'

I went back to nodding, hoping I did know.

'Well, when we speak of the Power, we use a capital P. All right?'

'Right.'

'We get the Power, with its capital P, from the Little People. And every willow has its own family. Down here, the willows are so good there's a whole congregation. It's not the same everywhere. They used to have lots in France, but now they've mostly gone again.'

'Why?'

'Because in France they had the Great War. There were so many bombs and bullets they killed most of the willows and so the Little People had to go. You can't stay if the only place you can live in is got rid of. The bullets couldn't hurt Little People, but their trees were gone. Probably by the end of this war there'll be none left anywhere there's been bullets.'

'They could come here. There's three more willows over the other side of our place where there used to be a house.'

'Sorry, but those willows are already let, and some of them are a bit little.'

We sat glum, looking at the streamers. Every so often I had quick looks at Dotty to make sure she wasn't tricking me.

'Trouble is,' she said slowly, 'big boys come out here sometimes, shooting for rabbits. If they don't shoot a rabbit, they shoot the trees. Can you think what that does to them?'

'What about shooting at dead trees?'

'It's the same. Anyway, the birds live there. We get the Power from the Little People. But only through the trees.'

'How?'

'If you stand in the willows, you'll find out. First, it fills your head and then your ears and nose and, through your nose, your breathing. And it keeps going down until your feet are tingling with it and you feel your hair start to feel crispy. Then you know. You become with the willow. So, if you should shoot the willow, you really shoot part of yourself and me and all of us. We are all of the willow. And it's here on the mound beside the creek where you talk to the willows and start the getting of the Power.'

I was starting to fidget, crossing my legs and hoping we could think about moving on. 'Does it take a long time to finish getting this Power?'

'Sometimes. Why?'

'What if you have to do something else, very badly?'

'Such as?'

'What if you have to go to the lavatory?'

'You have to wait.'

'What if you can't wait?'

'Men!' she said quietly. 'Well, off you go. But don't do a wet on the mound.'

I jumped up and started into the thickest streamers of the willow. I didn't get there.

She started screaming at me. 'Charlie, I mean Michael. Never, never, never, never do a wet on a willow. That's terrible disrespect. That's like doing a wet in church. Do it over there on the thistles. I'll look the other way if you like.'

'Doesn't matter. I can stand the other way round.'

She waited for me to stop and return. 'That's good,' she said as I sat down again. 'You'll feel more comfortable now.'

'Do all the trees have Little People?' I asked as if nothing had interrupted our talk and I could sound a bit more grown-up.

'Every one. Has to be that way. That's the rule. They need each other. The trees have great character, but they can't really move, so they need someone who will run messages and find out what's happening in town. And the Little People need the trees, like we need grandmothers. That's why. They're of the willow also.'

'Do the Little People live under here?' I asked patting the ground between us.

'Yes.'

'Then, if I got a crowbar and shovel, could I dig down to them?'

Dotty laughed and she sounded just like my auntie. 'Oh dear,' she said as if to herself. 'You've been listening to too many grown-ups. Of course you can't dig down to them. Even the deepest well couldn't find them. Trying to dig down to them is like trying to look into a house by scratching into the paint on the back door. Especially when all you've got to do is turn the handle.'

I nodded, hoping she might think I understood. 'Why haven't I seen one before?' I asked.

'Because you've been with people who only care for things, that's why. Besides, your dad, like my dad, is at the front. Every day I wish my daddy was home and I could show him my willow and he could play with us here among the Little People.'

'Does he believe?'

Dotty nodded.

'How do you know?'

'Because he told me so. Before he went to Africa, he got me to ask the Little People to keep him safe.'

'Do they do that sort of thing?'

'I hope so. When I sit here and put my hands on the mound, I can smell my daddy. You smell a bit like my daddy.'

I gave her a little push on the shoulder and the cry on her face stopped; the tear went dry.

'You must promise to keep the faith, Charlie Dyer – the Old Faith,' she said. 'Promise?'

I nodded and told her I'd keep my promise. It worried me a bit, because I wasn't very good at keeping promises.

'If you do, you'll have everything you ever wanted.'

'Like what?'

'Anything and everything.'

'But like what? Tell me something I could get.'

'Pick something. Would you like gold?'

I said yes, that gold would be something special. I knew my grandmother would like it. She could polish it every Saturday morning with Brasso.

'Then sit here a moment and I'll say a little prayer to the tree.'

I watched as she closed her eyes, made the Sign of the Cross like a

Catholic and said, 'Dear gentle tree of a hundred thousand weepings, help my daddy and Michael's father come home. Turn all the bullets into shop-made lollies and keep crying for the Little People.' She made the Sign of the Cross again and opened her eyes. 'Now I'll get you some gold.'

I said that that would be a good idea. We stood up and she turned around three times on the spot, crossed herself again, put both her arms out in front like someone pretending to sleep walk. Then, with her in front, peeping through her eyelashes like kids do when we play blind man's buff, we walked from the willow to a hawthorn bush about a cricket pitch away. She looked down at the ground and put her hands together as if praying again.

On the other side of the hawthorn bush, she reached in and snapped off a thorn. 'I tell you what. At school I'll call you Charlie. But at your place I'll call you Mick. Is that all right?'

I was going to nod, but she kept on.

'Just now, squeeze up the top of your thumb till it goes big.'

I squeezed and suddenly Dotty stabbed me with the thorn, and a little bubble of blood oozed out shiny.

I didn't cry out. I was nearly six and I knew I shouldn't let on to pain. 'Why?' was all I asked.

'Just so you won't forget. Now bring me a stone.'

'Where from?'

'From around here. Pick up the first one that draws you.'

I walked a few strides to a stone lying there with lots of others. It was round and the top was almost covered with grey lichen. I took it back to her.

She lay her hand on it and smiled. 'First off,' she said, 'there's gold in that one.'

'How do you know?'

'Because of the Power.'

She took the stone and pushed it under the thorn bush. 'Get a few more.'

I carried several. Not all of them had gold. Some she touched and rejected and those I tossed as far as I could. Some were as big as loaves and some were only as big as buns. I worked till we had a little pile of rocks under the bush.

'That'll do,' she said, and we stood there looking down at the little cairn.

I was starting to sweat. Picking up gold is hard work after a while. My thumb still hurt.

'There's enough gold there to take care of your entire future. You'll never have to worry now. If you have a rainy-day, you won't have to worry. You'll always know you can come back here, get your gold and that'll be the end of your problem.'

I looked at her round face as she stared into the bush and I knew I had met yet another great person in my life. Someone I would be unable to explain in a letter home to my mother, or even to my grandmother. But I knew she'd always be my very best, number one, special best friend.

That day of enlightenment was more than seventy years ago. Perhaps in some strange way, my thumb still hurts. I can't feel it, but it hurts.

For the next few years at least, Dotty stayed with the Power. Then the war ended and after that my dad came back from the front and I left the willows and went back to Sydney.

Dotty's father didn't come back. He stayed at the front even though the war was over. She said he was sleeping with the last of the Little People in France. They needed him there.

The day before I left Candelo, Dotty and I sat together on the mound and I cried a bit, because I knew her father would never come home to see the willows. I promised Dotty before the willows, and with both hands on the mound, that I would keep the Faith, no matter what happened, no matter what others might say.

Since then, I have thought of Dotty a hundred thousand times. I've seen the memory of her in willows in other people's gardens, in parks and from car and train windows in many strange countries. I've kept my promise to her. I've broken many promises to others, mostly promises I wanted to keep. But with her, it's different. I've never done a wet on a willow; I've never shot a willow – or any tree. And in the business of life, I've taken lots of risks, always knowing there was no real risk, because deep in the very keep of me, I knew the gold was always there, as Dotty said, 'against a rainy day'.

There's been lots of damp days, a fair few of drizzle, and once or twice I thought the dams might burst and wash me and my sore thumb to oblivion. But it didn't happen. Candelo has stayed with me through Dotty. I need to hope that Dotty is still as she was, that she is still of the Old Faith, that she is still of the willows, still of the Power with a capital P.

The Sewing Machine

Candelo

I heard her stamping up the steps, heard the wire screen door squeal open and Grandma exploded into the kitchen. I knew it was all over.

'Michael!' she said. So it was more than all over. When I was good, she called me Mick.

'You just come here this minute.'

But I couldn't really move. She already had me by the top of my ear. She was very strong, my grandma. I wasn't so sure about my ear.

Tommy Vigal at school, he said that his grandmother had gotten so angry that one day, she'd ripped his ear right off. But then she'd sewn it back on again, in case he had to wear glasses when he grew up. His mother wore glasses.

'Michael, you just come and explain to me the mystery of them disappearing strawberries.'

I was dragged by the ear down the back. Actually, I had just been down-the-back by myself. Our rickety old lavatory was called down-the-back. You didn't use it unless you had to sit down. Otherwise, you just stood up round-the-back.

That day was when I really saw the new strawberry garden right against the fence. I'd never seen strawberries growing before. Grandma must have got the plants and put them in while I was at school, the day before. In Sydney, strawberries came in little boxes and always red. These ones were green, but some were a bit yellow. The yellowy ones tasted better than the green ones, but I kept eating in case I'd miss a good one. In the end, they were all gone; all down inside me.

But they didn't stay there long. There was that awful wriggly feeling you get when you've been rocking about, more than five stops on a tram, and up they came. All of them right in front of the lavatory door. That was when I should have stood up and gone around the back. But I didn't. I ran back up the path.

Back in the kitchen, Grandma could see I'd been sick. She went to see for herself. That's why she'd exploded back into the kitchen. And just after that, we both went down the back. And there, for all Australia to see, was the green and gold of half-chewed strawberries spread out all over the path.

I tried to explain, what I believed to be the truth, that a whole family of big magpies had flown down and done all that because I had thrown my school bag at them the day before.

I don't think she heard me because, to keep my ear on, I had to let the rest of me follow Grandma up the path. We went into and through the kitchen, down the hall and stopped at the sickroom.

I hated the sickroom. You felt awful just standing outside. Everything was wrong with it. The floor squeaked and one wardrobe covered up half the window. Anything Grandma didn't like was squeezed into the sick room. There were garden pots and bundles of things, empty suitcases, hat boxes, an old bird cage, a rolled-up tent with wooden poles, an old meat safe, a German gramophone that surrendered when the war started, a sewing machine you treadle with your feet, and there was the big bed with things pushed underneath. There wasn't enough room for fresh air. You felt sick as soon as you went in.

'Grandma, I want to go down-the-back.'

'Get into bed, you little monkey, and not a squeak out of you.'

It was hard to climb up onto the big bed, but being lifted up by the ear helped a bit.

'Now you lie still. Don't move. Don't you move till I come and let you up.' And she was gone again.

But I did move. I wanted to go round-the-back, down-the-back. I turned face-down, but it didn't help. I lay on my back and crossed my feet over, then my knees, and I remembered two of the boys at school talking about tying knots. I tried a sort of bending. That didn't work either. My thing burned. It hurt. The hurt wasn't so bad I was in tears – like crying – but I could feel a hot little tear starting to run down the inside of my leg onto my best pyjamas.

Just then, I heard Grandma drag out the big bucket from the kitchen cupboard and she went out. I heard her footsteps and the bucket, banging down-the-back. I jumped out of bed and scrambled to the window. I knew exactly what to do. If I stood on a suitcase, I could lift the window open and do it outside. No one would ever know. I grabbed the handles on the window and tried to push up. It wouldn't budge. Someone had nailed the window shut. Probably to stop the Germans if they tried to get in. I clambered up onto the windowsill to pull-push the top window down. It moved, but only a bit. I looked at the top of the wardrobe. Even if I could climb up there, I'd have to stand on my hands to get that part of me out the window. Even then, I'd need to stand on one hand because I'd need the other hand to get things ready and stop my pyjama pants falling up. What to do? Peter Shooks at school, he said he'd have no trouble because he could have stood on the windowsill, held onto the top of the window with one hand and, with his other hand, stretched his thing up past the two windows, then out through the opening at the top, around the loquat tree outside and pointed it down the drain. I knew I couldn't. And, what with all that stretching, what if my thing ripped off? I'd have to run down to Tommy Vigal's and get his grandmother to sew it back on again. And what if there was bleeding – on my best pyjamas? I knew I couldn't do it. Besides when everything's urgent, you haven't got time to try things.

I get down and rummage under the bed for that pot thing. There isn't one. I try the wardrobe. There are lots of pots, but they're garden ones and they've all got big round holes in the bottom. I scramble all over the floor. Nothing. I look under the sewing machine. Just cardboard boxes full of cotton reels and things. But as I stand up again, I see. The sewing machine has four drawers, two on each side.

The top one on that side is full of bits and pieces; but the second, the second one, is empty.

I hear the wire screen door squeal open again. Grandma is coming back. She bangs down the bucket on the porch. She comes through the kitchen. She is halfway down the hall as I, very carefully, slide the drawer shut.

By the time she was in the sickroom, I was in bed – sound asleep.

She walked in and sniffed. 'Michael! You wet the bed?'

'No, Grandma. I don't do that, not since I started school.'

She walked out again, saying the room needed a good airing.

I stayed there all morning. Easy. The panic was gone.

About lunchtime, she said I could get up and go back to my own room. She said she'd bring me a sandwich and she called me Mick. I knew things would be all right again. Well, they'd be all right until she wanted to use the sewing machine.

For the next six months, all through that long-hot summer, I never went near the sickroom in case Grandma saw me and twigged what had happened. I never ate strawberries again either, not even red ones.

Then, one Saturday, Grandma went into Candelo to shop. I had my chance. As soon as she was past Vigal's dairy, I went into the sickroom with the bucket.

I plonked the bucket down next to the sewing machine and slid the drawer open. I couldn't believe what I didn't see. Things were wrong. It certainly was the same drawer. But the drawer was empty. How could it be it empty? But it was. There wasn't even a little puddle in the far corner.

I don't know how it got empty. I didn't do it. I don't think my grandma did it. She would have let me know. Nothing happened. No one ever knew. But it became something I wouldn't forget, an episode that changed me. I still don't like strawberries. And I don't like anything like a sickroom, and I don't like them fancy new sewing machines in their shiny plastic boxes that do all sorts of flashy stitches. They don't have drawers.

The Wireless

Candelo

In Candelo, the news on the wireless was always fun. It was my best thing before going to bed, and the best part of that was all the sparks. The news coming out of the wireless lasted much longer than the sparks, but it wasn't nearly so much fun. The sparks lit up most of the kitchen.

After tea and the washing-up, we always sat and listened to the news. It was something we had to do. We would both sit in front of the stove, with the fire box open, and we wound balls of wool for knitting.

The khaki-coloured wool came from the Red Cross and it was for knitting socks and scarves for soldiers at the front.

The wool came in what Grandma called skeins. They were a messy loop, tied at both ends. My job was to untie the loops and put a hand in at each end and stretch the skein open. With a lot of fiddling, Grandma would find an end and start rolling a ball. The skein was always a tangle and sometimes it took most of our time just to get one ball.

At six o'clock, Grandma closed the blackout curtains, turned up the kerosene lamp and advanced on the wireless. That was my secret fun for the night. The wireless was big and sat on the top of a big, wind-up gramophone. The gramophone was taller than me and covered up the copper wires that hung down behind. Grandma was frightened of those wires. She never said so, but she was. On the end of the two wires hung two strong clips with teeth. They had to be opened by hand and forced to bite onto the two poles of the big tractor battery on the floor.

Grandma would grab a plug in each hand, squeeze open the jaws of the clips and stab at the battery terminals. She never got it right first off, and each time she scraped the battery, there was a shower of sparks that lit the room. But eventually she did make good contacts.

We heard the news in the morning as well. But it wasn't so much fun. The sparks were better at night. The room had to be dark.

When the news was over – and it seemed the news was never good news – it was easy to unplug. All you had to do was grab the wires and pull. You got sparks, but not so many. And only one lot.

While the news was on, Grandma sat looking into the fire with the wool in her lap and sometimes swearing at the Nazis. Whenever I said anything against the Germans, she would tell me off. In Candelo, it seemed everyone but the two of us was German. Grandma said all of them had German names. So it was the Nazis who were the bad ones. Most of the young men in Candelo were in France, at the front – fighting Germans.

In the mornings, I had to stand while Grandma combed my hair for school. And she would listen to the wireless. Until the news was over, she would just keep combing and combing. Actually, it hurt. In those days, I had tight curly hair and she had a fine-tooth comb. It was a bad combination.

Grandma always muttered about the war and what she wanted to do with a man called Hitler. However, one day it was different.

I was standing to attention wanting the combing to stop. I wanted to be in the playground before the bell went. Grandma suddenly tensed and stopped combing. At first, she just gripped me gently by the hair. The news went on and it seemed she stopped breathing. Suddenly, she tightened her grip on my hair, shook me and started to lift me off the floor. She screamed swear words at the wireless, shook my head from side to side then wrapped her arms around my whole head and jammed my face against her front.

She held me so tight I couldn't breathe. I started to wriggle and with that she let me go and put the comb down on the table. She sat down, buried her face in her hands and kept on swearing the same word. 'Bastards!' It was a word I knew, but was never allowed to use. She kept on saying it and was more angry than I had ever known anyone to be so angry.

The kids at school didn't know why she behaved like that. I thought it must have been the Nazis again. They were always causing trouble in the news.

I asked Miss Thompson about it. I told her about the combing. She just looked sad, gave me a hug and said she'd tell me another day. But she never did and other worries came along instead.

We lived in Candelo another year or so. By then, Grandma was restless again and we went back to Sydney. I was to go back and live with my mother.

Some twenty years after that, I learned the truth.

Grandma was dying in hospital. I'd never thought that such a thing could happen. I hadn't seen her for more than a year and when I walked into her hospital room, her eyes lit up and she reached out to touch me.

My auntie was there and just to make sure Grandma knew who I was she said, 'Here's your not-so-little Brian.'

Grandma looked at me and tried to say the word 'Mick'.

There was a radio next to her bed and though it wasn't turned on, the sight of it sparked the memory. It had electricity plugged in from the wall. There would be no sparks. Just the news.

I wondered if I should ask.

She looked at me almost unable to speak. However, her look said, 'What would you like to know?'

'Grandma, remember Candelo?'

She smiled and nodded.

'There was one day you were combing my hair.'

She nodded again.

'You were very angry.' I wondered if I should go on; a tear was rolling down her face.

'Was it because of the Nazis?'

She tried to shake her head and squeezed my hand.

'Why then?'

She tried to pull me closer and I put my face on the pillow next to her. She had huge difficulty to make a sound. I heard one word. It was hard to decipher through a fog of hisses and breaths. 'Cap,' she said, 'Capit.'

Suddenly the sparks showered in my brain and I understood. 'Capitulation?'

She nodded and relaxed.

I said the rest, 'The capitulation of France.' She nodded, turned her face and tried to kiss me. I knew it was to say sorry. I should have known.

My grandfather had died in France during the Great War. A war before my time. A war that even brought Grandma and me together in Australia. My grandfather was her hero-husband and father of her eight children. The seventh was my mother. It was because of his death that Grandma hated France, and she hated all armies.

My grandfather was a sapper, tunnelling under a hill in Arras to blow up the German defences. The sappers worked in shifts underground. The shift before my grandfather's had come up saying that the Germans had set charges on their side and had left their digging. Down there in the dark, each side could hear the others working. My grandfather's group refused to go down. Their officer, an eighteen-year-old public school boy only the week before, drew his pistol and ordered the men down. If they refused, they'd be charged and shot for desertion.

My grandfather and his pals shouldered their tools and went down singing 'It's a long way to Tipperary'. They were barely underground when the German charges fired. My grandfather and his team were blown to smithereens and buried.

Grandma always remembered the name of the young English officer. She said he'd died only a few days later. Many of the young officers only lasted a few days. I think Grandma had leaned to forgive the young officer, but there was one thing she never forgave. The English army, when they finally paid her my grandfather's last rewards for his service to King and Country, subtracted one shilling for the cost of his burial sheet.

That was when she had decided to leave England. The shilling – for a burial sheet he never had – rankled with her for the rest of her life. She developed an abiding hatred of the military mentality. Any mention of the word France brought the bitterness to the surface once again. She had been cheated by the British army and while she was combing my hair she was let down by the French.

I sat with her, but we had already closed our wonderful times together. She lived two more days and I moved up another generation.

My generation is populated by news junkies. We just have to listen to the news. I still must. The stories are marginally happier, but the fun is gone. The reception is better and the sets are smarter and smaller – but I miss the sparks.

Drifting Off

Candelo, 1942

Miss Thompson was saying something about a man had ten oranges. I tried to listen. Trouble was, I knew that soon she would say that if he took two oranges away, how many would he have left? I also knew I could do it on my fingers, but it was the number ten that made me start to drift off. You see, we didn't use the number ten for anything. Not that I could think of anyway. We used the numbers six and twelve and it was easier to say 'half a dozen and a dozen'. And if a man had twelve oranges he wouldn't take away two, he'd take away six. That was when I really drifted off a bit further.

It all depends on what you already know. We had six strands of wire on all our fences and all of them around dry-looking paddocks. Grandma said there was a limit as to how long we could go without rain. She said we needed rain within six weeks. There it was again – half a dozen. No one waited five weeks for anything. Besides, you wouldn't say five of something. You'd say a handful.

Miss Thompson kept on about the oranges when I really drifted off. Actually, I used to go off pretty regular. I think that's why Miss Thompson moved me away from the windows – right into the middle. But I drifted off just the same. Miss Thompson was still talking about the man with ten oranges and if he got one more, how many then? I didn't really hear the answer; I had already drifted into the big paddock where we kept the horses. I always drift there. I think it's because I like horses. But this time it was clear, I could see everything, even the grass. It was like after a frosty morning. I got clear pictures of everything. But there was a difference. This time there was a sort of house. It was wooden, a weatherboard house. It was one of those old houses, but without a front veranda. It had a door in the middle and a window on each side and a rusty tin roof. I knew there really was no such thing as that house, but it was there in my drifting.

I walked up to the front door and pulled it open. I moved back a bit, but nothing fell out. The house was full from the floor to the ceiling with oranges. Not tens, but grosses of dozens. They should have started to tumble out, but they didn't. I reached in and took one. Still the others didn't fall. They should have. If they'd been stooks of hay, they would have. If you pull out a bottom sheaf, the top ones tumble down all over you and it takes all day to pick out the itchy bits out from inside your shirt. But the oranges stayed put.

I dropped the first orange on the ground behind me and got a second one. Still they didn't fall. I started pulling them out fast and throwing them over my shoulder behind me. Pretty soon I could stand in the doorway boxed in with yellow oranges. I turned around to look outside. All the oranges I had thrown out had vanished. They should have been all over the place waiting for Miss Thompson to take away two, so we could count the rest. But there was nothing there, just dry grass.

I picked out another orange and watched as I threw. I saw it all the way till it hit the ground. Then it just disappeared – just wasn't there any more. I knew then there was something special about this house of oranges. These oranges were somehow special to me. But I couldn't just throw them away. For all that, something told me that I would throw one away whenever I did something. And if I threw one away, how many would I have left? And would I have to subtract one if I didn't stop drifting in school? Even when Miss Thompson didn't know I was drifted off. And I reckoned that one day I would hold the last orange in my hand. That would give me the right answer.

Just then, Miss Thompson looked hard at me and asked that if she were to subtract three oranges, how many would I have left? I hadn't really come back, so I told her not to worry because there were at least four rooms, still full, right to the roof. And if there was a bathroom and laundry on the closed-in back veranda, there would be enough for a long, long time. She looked at me sort of soft. She nodded and asked me where on earth I had been. I told her in the new house I had just discovered. She smiled a little and some of the bigger girls in the class giggled. She made them be quiet. She kept nodding up and down, saying nothing, but looking at me. Then after a bit she asked us all to take out our reading books.

We opened up at Penelope's Tapestry. That morning I really found out about Penelope. That's when I learned that all those old stories really mean something. Penelope had stitches. She worked at them all day. But at night, she took some away. Sometimes she subtracted all of them; how many would she have left? The answer was easy. There were none left. But she knew what she was doing. She learned all about stitches. I learned all about oranges. We were a pair and I never forgot.

Fifty-odd years later, I was at a funeral in Bundanoon. A friend of mine, Sid, had died suddenly. Later on, I was told he had a heart valve that just jammed shut. Well, Bundanoon was a small place and it fell to everyone to chip in and help out.

The local cabinetmaker, called Fred, drove the family to the cemetery and he and I helped the undertaker lower the coffin into the ground. Neither of us had done such a job before and we whispered together nervously.

The cabinetmaker asked Sid's age. I said he was sixty.

'And how old are you?'

I told him I was fifty-nine.

The situation set me off. I started to drift. I heard the carpenter say it was hardly worth my while going home and he tried stop a nervous giggle by talking.

'Do you reckon he'd had some sort of warning, say ten years ago?'

By then I had drifted right off. I heard Miss Thompson, back in school, asking the same sort of question. I didn't really answer. I had drifted further off and there I was back in the same horse paddock. The little old-fashioned house was still there, but I didn't open the door. This time, there was a deep grave in front of the house. It was open. I looked in and saw Sid's coffin in the bottom.

I heard the carpenter going on with the same problem. 'He must have had something,' he said.

I shook my head. 'No,' I said quietly to him and Miss Thompson. 'He just ran out of oranges.'

Granny

Grandma wasn't the only grandmother in my life. My uncle Tom and my auntie Tessy had a mother called Granny. Everyone loved Granny. I don't remember any of her names, but I can instantly recall an image of her, the little lady, forever in black, a laugh-a-minute lady who cared for everyone in the world around her. For me, she was a person of some mystery. She could read the cards and foretell the future. It was considered by both my mother and grandmother that Granny's fortune telling was in line with her Irish Catholicism. Grandma said Granny was descended from the Druids. Whatever other women thought of her skills and religion, they all rushed to her for sure-fire answers to family problems.

All the time I knew Granny, she was poor. She had always been poor since her childhood back in the mists of the Celtic twilight. She had grown up a laughing, barefooted strip of a girl running around in the bogs, singing Gaelic songs and pouring down blessings on her friends and relatives.

Granny was a fervent Catholic. Her life and interests were guided by appeals to her favourite saints and her daily devotion to the Virgin Mary. Granny burned candles. She burned candles in solidarity with those around her in need of help. She burned candles for Catholics, Protestants and any other group she heard about.

She even burned candles for the sick dog next door. When the dog recovered, she burned another candle to give thanks. I doubt the dog's owner ever knew how the recovery came about.

Throughout the war, Granny burned candles for the safe return of my father, and, I learned a few years later, she also regularly burned candles for me that I might do well at school. Australian candle makers did very well out of Granny.

Not that Granny had never had prospects. At eighteen, she married a young man of excellent prospects. At last her future seemed assured and prosperous. Granny was in love with her man and they planned an exciting life together. Like many Irish couples, they felt that prospects might be better elsewhere. So after the wedding, they sailed for Australia and for the following weeks they enjoyed their honeymoon and, for the first and last time in their lives, had nothing to do except enjoy each other's company. All her life, Granny looked back on the trip from Ireland to Sydney as a memory of a wonderful dream she must have had.

On the ship, with plenty of opportunity and, according to Granny, with God's help, they conceived their first baby.

Her handsome young man was a qualified stonemason, at a time when his trade was highly regarded and his income higher than most tradesmen. It was even customary for a stonemason to wear a bowler hat. Bricklayers usually wore a cap – or whatever they could lay their hands on.

Despite his status, his prospects didn't last. One month after they arrived in Sydney, he developed a severe kidney disease and he virtually never worked again. They clung together, loving and glad to have each other. So glad, they managed to have four more children. So Granny became the breadwinner, mother and carer in one.

My service to Granny was as a runner to the local SP bookie. Granny loved to bet. She would bet on anything – even the proverbial two flies walking up the windowpane. She'd bet me threepence that her fly would get farther up than mine. She'd supply the threepenny bit. If she won, she took back the little coin. She usually lost, which meant I kept the money. It is the only form of gambling in which I was successful. On Saturday mornings, she would give me sixpence along with the name of a horse, or a greyhound, she fancied and I'd run round to Mr Winston's back veranda. Then I'd run back to Granny and we'd listen to the race on the wireless.

My mother loved Granny and would try to talk her out of

gambling what little money she had. Many times I heard my mother say, 'Granny, don't give your money to those awful men.'

Granny would always reply, 'God love you, Kit, but how can I expect God to help me if I don't make an effort myself?'

I think this logic escaped my mother, but my grandmother understood. Grandma had a sweet contempt for people who rushed to prayers asking for help, 'When they've done nothing to deserve it.' Grandma had also lost a young husband.

Granny would laugh over stories that filled me with near horror. She often laughed over her last 'lying-in'. Her youngest baby arrived sooner than expected and Granny managed everything with only the help of the lady next door. As the baby was halfway out, the lady next door laughed and admonished Granny for not having read of the event in the cards. As soon as the little boy was free and the umbilical cord tied off with string and cut with a pair of well boiled scissors, Granny explained that the cards were an inexact science.

For some months, Granny had put penny coins aside for when the baby arrived. Half an hour after little Vincent was born, she called the two girls of seven and five years old, gave them the coins and sent them off to get a chicken from the 'ham and beef shop'. She knew she would be unable to get up and arrange a meal for four people.

She waited for the cold chicken to arrive. The girls returned happy with their choice. They brought back a cheap, but fully feathered squawking, nice, plump, but well and truly still-alive chicken.

Granny would laugh as she described how she lay back on the edge of the bed with her newborn baby beside her, and had the girls spread newspaper on the floor beside her. She then leaned over the side and with the bread knife, dispatched the chicken. She had their only large saucepan of boiling water brought in and had the girls help her pluck all the feathers and gut the chicken. For me, her episode was a dreadful story of new life and death in the one room at one time. But Granny would laugh and thank God for all His help.

By the time I had been living in London for a year or so. I had developed an antagonism to Christianity. But I kept it quiet. Why disappoint others if there's nothing to win? However, at a strange confluence of events, my mother wrote to tell me that Granny was still burning candles for me to ensure a safe return to Australia. When I read about Granny, I remembered my favourite story of her famous splurge on the dogs. She had been told of a good bet, but this time she was given a sure thing in the last race.

'Put your shirt on him,' said the man who had inside info.

At the races, Granny went carefully. She had put her return bus fare in a special pocket of her purse and her betting money in the main section. There were many races and Granny fancied the look of a dog in each race. Unfortunately, she hadn't consulted the cards before she left. None of her dogs won.

Then came the last race with her sure thing looking good. She opened her purse to the sickening realisation that all her betting money was gone. Only her return fare remained. She looked hard and long at the big coin. She was tempted, but logic told her it was a long walk home. It would be dawn before she got there. The dogs were approaching the starting boxes as Granny reviewed her options. It was either walk home, or the possibility of luxurious living for a whole week. She looked at the odds. Her dog was fourteen to one. Another dog was favourite. Never before had she had such a chance. The temptation was powerful and Granny had to cross herself, to put temptation well and truly behind. She would watch the race instead and get the bus home.

She was holding the two-shilling coin in her hand as the dogs were readied. And in that instant, two things happened at once. The race started just as Granny turned and started running towards the nearest bookie. She said she ran like the wind. So did her dog.

The bookie saw her coming and laughed. 'What dog?' he shouted.

Granny turned and saw the race about to end with her dog well in the lead. As she reached the bookie with the coin outstretched to him, she forgot the dog's name. 'The one in front,' she shouted back.

'You're right, love,' the bookie told her. He couldn't stop laughing. By the time he took her money, the race was over. The bookie returned her two shillings along with a fist full of coins. She showered him with devout blessings.

There were many more stories, but that was my favourite.

I had grown tired of London's weather and decided on escape. I was off to sunny Spain to write the Great Australian Novel. Actually, I think it is still there. But like Granny, I got inside information. A petrol company provided a map of the most direct and cheapest route.

I had a small Renault 4CV, which I drove onto the ferry at Dover, and off again at Calais. For the whole day, I drove south along the west coast of France. The next day, I crossed the Pyrenees, though not in one go.

Near the mountain peak, the road reminded me of wartime Australia. It was unpaved, corrugated and occasionally the recipient of small rockfalls from the mountain side above. I wondered if the trip was worth it. Several times I had to stop and remove small boulders from the carriageway. No cars passed me in either direction.

Somewhere near the top, a signpost indicated a possible diversion. It read, 'Lourdes 25kls'.

I was driving slowly anyway, but at that point I thought of Granny. Before that moment, I had no idea where Lourdes actually lay. All I knew was that the Virgin Mary had appeared to a girl called Bernadette, somewhere in France. Bernadette later became a much venerated saint. I turned left, which is not a bad strategy for anyone in doubt, and headed for Lourdes and something to send to Granny.

Lourdes was dreadful, ugly and disgusting. It was a market of Christian kitsch. It reminded me of Woy Woy without the glamour. The once-Catholic schoolboy from Candelo in me was revolted. But just the same, I wanted to buy something Catholic for Granny. I was overwhelmed with offers of first-customer-discounted bargains.

I ended up with a Rosary made of plastic. The salesman assured me the beads were made of Lourdes crystal and each contained a droplet of holy water from the sacred grotto of Saint Bernadette. I didn't believe a word of it, but I bought them – three blessings and all.

I never saw Granny again. She died long before I returned to Australia. But I did hear of her. Not long after my holy visit to Lourdes, my mother went to a family funeral.

After the ceremony, Granny came running up to her bubbling over with excitement. She grabbed my mother's arm in both her hands. 'Oh, Kit,' she started. 'You've got no idea. That wonderful Mick of yours. He's the most wonderful boy in all my life. Do you know, he sent me the most wonderous present I have ever received. The best ever in all my life. That boy of yours drove all the way to Lourdes and the holy grotto and he got a special Rosary just for me. It's made of Lourdes crystal and each bead has a drop of holy water from the sacred grotto of Saint Bernadette. It's the best present I have ever got. And do you know, Kit? Since I got it, I've backed three winners.'

Two Sides

Chatswood, 1946

My father had been working non-stop in his vegetable garden. Grandma said it was the only way he could get over his time in the war. He was endlessly picking beans and cucumbers, watering lettuce plants and forever weeding. He said that every family should be able to live off their own backyard. I respected his ability to grow anything. I also did well from his efforts. While he was at work during the week, I quietly gleaned a few vegetables here and there, filled the bucket and hawked the fruits of his labour around the streets. I probably earned more from his garden than he earned from his job in the navy.

That Sunday, my mother leaned out the kitchen window and called him in for afternoon tea. As he entered the kitchen, he complained that some of his crop was missing. I decided to stay out of the room, but within earshot. My mother turned off the primus stove, filled the teapot and produced a plate of cupcakes. That gave them an advantage. I had to go in.

But things went well. He started to fume about the coal miners and their 'Communist strike'.

My mother tried to settle him down and said something about the miners might have a good reason.

This did not have the desired effect for her, but it suited me. He'd already forgotten his missing vegetables and started on about how it all started back in the days of Jack Lang and Lang's sympathy for the workers, how Australia was about to be run by the Russians. He said it wouldn't be long before Stalin took over the New South Wales government. Ben Chifley came in for little more than scowls, and if

Chifley had any guts at all, he'd call out the army and march the miners down the pits. After that, there'd be no more trouble and we'd just turn on the electric kettle and have a cup of tea whenever we wanted one. It all made sense and I tried to encourage him not to change the subject.

The next day was Monday and the first day of the September holidays. That meant my mother packed my suitcase, walked me to the tram stop and made sure I had the correct seat at the back, and I left to spend my holidays with Grandma.

It was a good trip. I only threw up once and a lady sitting next to me kept me supplied with Minties.

I walked up Saint Albans Street and talked to all the ladies who told me how much taller I was and how glad my grandma would be to see me.

Grandma was just making a cup of tea on her methylated spirit stove. It was a dangerous one-burner gadget which had no controls other than a metal hat which suffocated the flame once the kettle boiled.

Grandma offered me a cup of tea and a biscuit.

We sat down together and I told her it was a shame she had to use a spirit stove and it would all be fixed if only Mr Chifley had the guts to call out the army and march the miners down the pits.

It didn't have the desired effect.

Grandma turned on me. 'And who told you that?' she demanded . Her face turned into a furious red moon and she poked her finger into my chest. 'I bet that silvertail father of yours filled you up with all that tripe. What would he know about the mines? He's never been down a mine in his whole life. He wouldn't work in an iron lung. He wouldn't know work if it was served up with meat and three veg.'

Grandma settled down after that and I had to answer the usual questions about my mother and my sister. But I didn't settle down. My chest hurt a bit and I couldn't understand such fury, just because of something I said. How could two people who were so close to me not believe the same things. I wasn't sure I wanted to grow up. In truth, I don't believe I have.

Blackfella Charlie (Mr Rose)

Atherton Tableland, 1948

It was a rule in my family that you don't touch strangers. You certainly don't point your finger at anyone and you're in pretty serious trouble if you're caught staring.

But I'd never seen a black man up close before. His mahogany-coloured face was the same as naked natives in the National Geographic magazine, but it was his hands and hair that got me. His hair was white – well, a yellowy white – and hung around his face in long, floppy curls. The curls joined up with a white beard to frame a face as shiny as if he had spent all morning buffing it up. But it was the hands that got me most. I had no idea that people could be two colours. The backs of his hands were black, almost blue black, but the palms were pink and I wanted to touch one of them, scratch it a bit, to test its colours close up.

Charlie held one of the stakes in his piebald hands turning it end on end, round on round as if it might change shape by itself.

'They're an inch by an inch, by a foot,' I said, trying to break into his problem.

He burst into an explosive giggle, but still played the stick about. I was surprised by the giggle, but pretended to concentrate on the stake. In truth, I was only staring at his hands.

'You wantim little axe?' I asked, hoping to be helpful; wanting to assure him I was prepared to speak his language.

'Does the boss have a tomahawk?'

Charlie glanced across the few yards of Bladey grass to the tin shed where my uncle squatted outside in the shade of the Master Chev. My uncle was talking loudly with the surveyor and the other man. The other man wore an army shirt and white moleskin trousers. There was a lull in their conversation as the surveyor looked from the mud map my uncle was scratching of the hills behind them.

'Uncle Ivan?' I started. 'Charlie needs the tomahawk.' I tried to sound polite.

'What did I hear you say, son?' my uncle demanded.

It was a voice I was coming to terms with. Sometimes, in company, he gave me orders. His voice would sound like an actor playing a sergeant in a war film. He asked me to repeat what I had just said and ended with a sort of angry laughter. I heard him say something to the surveyor that despite my size I was still only thirteen. The surveyor looked at me and nodded.

I started to repeat, but got no further than the word Charlie.

'How old are you?' my uncle barked.

'Almost fourteen,' I confirmed.

'Then for the next few years let me hear that man referred to by his name, which is…?'

'Mr Rose,' I answered and waited for the nod.

It came and I repeated the rephrased question. Mr Rose continued to look the stick over and giggled at all the carry-on.

My uncle shouted past me, 'In the shed, Charlie.' And then to me, 'You go with him, Mick, keep your eye on things.' And he went back to talking to the surveyor, laughing that he'd bought the survey pegs, blunt-ended, at half price.

As the two of us went into the shed to find the tomahawk, my uncle was saying something about making 'the old boong earn his handout'.

Inside the shed, all I could see of Charlie was his almost white shirt and his white hair. His face and the back of his hands disappeared into the sudden dark. Gradually my eyes adjusted and we searched about the walls for the tomahawk. The pungent smell from the timber studs was overpowering. My uncle had had the shed thrown up a few weeks before I arrived and the timbers had been sloshed over with creosote against termites. The morning outside was beginning to warm and the iron roof was beginning to crackle.

I found the tomahawk the moment the shouting started outside. Charlie gently leaned me aside as he rushed past out the doorway. Uncle was roaring like an upset bull, repeating the word 'taipan'. By the time I was through the door, uncle was jumping backwards like a frog in reverse. For the first time in the few weeks I had been there, I laughed. We used to do the same jump at school, down south, but we didn't make the same noise. I determined to try as soon as my uncle was out of sight. The surveyor and his mate stood where they had been squatting and Charlie sidled about between the car and uncle. He'd picked up a long-handled shovel from the truck and moved towards the snake. The snake didn't seem to be concerned. He was about six feet long and was slowly slithering through the ankle-high grass, heading in the direction of the shed.

'Quick time, Charlie!' roared my uncle. 'Get the bloody thing quick time.'

I looked at my uncle as if he were a stranger. I saw that he had a fat belly. He was jumping up and down on the spot now, but it seemed that only his legs flipped up and down while his round belly and head stayed roaring in mid air above them. For the second time in those few short weeks, I laughed again.

Charlie took a couple of steps and raised the shovel. My uncle bounced a few more times, but started to slow down like a yo-yo off balance. The shovel chopped down and Charlie stood to watch.

'Make sure of the bastard, Charlie,' shouted my uncle and his sergeant's voice filtered back again. 'Finish the bastard!'

'He's finished, boss,' said Charlie.

'Balls he's finished,' my uncle shouted back. 'Those bastards don't die till night time – not when he's wounded like that.' He inched forward, stretching to his full height to get a better look at the still writhing snake. 'He's a taipan all right. I saw the bastard.'

'No, boss, just a yella fella. Only eat a few of them imported rats that come with Captain Cook.'

'Don't tell me I don't know a taipan when I see one. Make sure the bastard's dead.'

Charlie giggled again and leaned down. Uncle started his bull-shouting again, but suddenly stopped the noise. His action changed to a jack-in-the-box. I tried not to laugh for the third time.

Charlie reached down and came up with the tail of the snake. From its tail to the break, up near its head, it hung still while the head and neck twirled about, its open mouth dripping blood. Charlie swung the snake above his head like a bull-roarer. Uncle made the noise for both of them and kept it going for about a minute after Charlie flicked his wrist and cracked the snake like a whip. The snake's head almost flew off. Charlie flung the twitching corpse onto the grass a few yards away and we went forward to inspect.

'That was a fantastic bit of work, Jacky,' said the surveyor's mate. He had a glow of admiration on his face and I felt I might make a new friend there.

'His name is Charlie Rose,' corrected my uncle. 'He does what's he's paid for – no use having a dog and barking yourself, is there?'

I wondered what he meant by barking, but the surveyor and his mate only swopped glances.

'You take the hatchet, Mick. Let Mr Rose carry the pegs. Everywhere you're told, you make sure the old man hammers in a peg. Savvy?'

Charlie picked up the bag of pegs and we fell in behind the other three. The surveyor went ahead with my uncle carrying the maps.

The surveyor's mate carried his elaborately numbered pole. The mate said something about the day getting hot already and we should have started just on dawn. 'Too plurry hot, Jacky?' he asked.

I winced, but when I looked at the mate, he was looking at Charlie in a friendly fashion.

'Too hot working in these parts,' said Charlie and he giggled again as if apologising.

'You reckon it's real blackfella country, Jacky?'

'Used to be,' laughed Charlie. 'But this young fella's mother bought it out.'

'She's my auntie,' I corrected.

'The lady doctor not your mother?'

'No, she's my auntie. She practises in Cairns and only comes up for weekends.'

'How long you been here then?' the mate asked me.

'Only a few weeks.'

'What's your old man do?'

'He's still in the navy. Works at the wireless station outside Canberra.'

About a hundred yards away, the surveyor set up his theodolite and waved to his mate. The mate shifted his pole about, inches at a time, and finally marked the earth with its foot. On the mark, Charlie stood his first peg and tried to belt it in. It wouldn't drive, the ground was too hard. He giggled again, knelt down and chopped a rough point onto the stake and managed to drive it into the ground.

'You're going to earn your bakky here, Jacky,' said the mate.

'Reckon,' confirmed Charlie quietly. 'The stakes are hard and the tomahawk is blunt – bad combination,' he added.

'His name is Charlie Rose,' I said quietly to the mate.

'It's all right, boss,' laughed Charlie.

'Sorry,' said the mate. 'I just spent three years in a Siamese POW camp and I like the sound of Jacky more than Charlie. But I don't want to hurt your feelings. I didn't come up here to hurt anyone.'

As we walked to the next position, the mate said something about Australia being big enough for everyone. Charlie laughed as he shouldered his sack of pegs. I offered to take the tomahawk, but he shrugged me off saying it gave him a better balance.

After two hours of walking, sharpening and hammering pegs, my fascination for Charlie's face and hands had eased off. I had walked back to the shed twice to collect more pegs and had taken drinks from the canvas bag. My legs were a maze of scratches from the rough grass and my face dried from the sun boring down like a poultice. I longed for lunchtime.

The second trip back with pegs, I met my uncle heading for the car. He was puffing like a bellows and he told me to hurry back, that I was 'holding up the works'. He wasn't right, because I could see Charlie on the next hill, holding an arm load of pegs while the surveyor and his mate sent semaphore signals to each other and the mate moved the pole.

When I reached them, Charlie had lost his giggle and moved from mark to mark like an old man grown weary of it all.

'How's it going, Charlie?' asked the mate.

'She's all right, Boss. Ground's a bit hard, that's all.'

He rubbed the sweat from his pink palm and I noticed a blister beside his thumb. It surprised me that a bushman and a blackfellow could get blisters. It made me feel a bit more equal, but I was sorry for him just the same.

About half an hour after that, Charlie nodded towards the shed. I looked over and saw my auntie's car pulling up. She got out and my uncle was there with her, waving his arm in the direction of all our pegs. I could sense him telling her how he'd supervised everything.

'What's a doctor want to grow here?' asked the mate.

'Peanuts,' I said as if I knew all about it.

'I suppose they need the contour planting,' he said wearily. 'You like peanuts, Charlie?'

'Not much, Boss. Not bad with a few beers or something. But you can't get a good feed with them. The kids like them, though.'

'The kids chew peanuts with a few beers, Charlie?'

'No, Boss. No beers. Besides, blackfellas can't drink, Boss.'

'You like a beer or two, Charlie?'

'Sure, Boss. Best thing your mob brought in.'

'Then we'll have a few quiet beers together, Charlie, when there's no one about. How's that?'

'Sure, Boss,' and he raised a giggle again and wiped his forehead with his index finger and flicked the sweat onto the ground just as the car horn blasted out for lunch.

We picked up our gear and headed back. By the time we reached the cars, my aunt had arranged everything. She had organised my uncle into putting up a tarp with a few poles. Under that, in the shade, she had spread first the ground sheet, then the table cloth and most of the lunch. She was putting out the buttered bread onto paper plates and she discreetly held everything in her fingertips. She smiled at me as I went with the others to the water basin to wash our hands.

I liked my aunt. She was the point of reference in my family. She was a doctor, an eye doctor, had been to an English university and had lots of money. You could tell that by the way she spoke and the way she always wore good clothes. Even up there, she wore gloves.

When I'd first arrived in Cairns, she was wearing her good clothes from first thing in the morning and gone straight to her surgery after breakfast. My uncle and I sat around waiting for the local lady to come and clean the place up and make the beds.

She'd done something to her hair. It wasn't that it was short, but that it was a funny yellow colour. My father, her brother, had impressed on me many times that I must never comment on what people did with their clothes or their hair, in fact anything. But there had been a comment between my grandmother and father, that people didn't trust lady surgeons with grey hair. My grandma had given a sort of snort and has said something quietly that it was a pity that with all that so-called breeding and all that money, my aunt couldn't have done better for herself in the way of a husband.

That comment had stuck in my memory like a bit of apple sticks in your throat every time you get tram-sick. I wondered if the peanuts would be the start of doing something better for herself.

Charlie used the bucket last and washed not only hands and arms, but his face and neck as well. There were towels beside the basin, but Charlie didn't get one. I offered him mine.

He went to take it, but glanced towards the others and shook his head. 'Never learned to use one,' he laughed.

I started to wish he wouldn't giggle all the time. There was never a joke and I got tired of laughing just to go along with him. I waited for him to come back with me under the tarp, but he hung back.

'You go, Boss, I'll be over later,' he said. He dried his face on the belly of his shirt and sat against the outside wall of the shed.

'Why won't Mr Rose come with us?' I asked as I sat on the grass beside the picnic.

'That because he's been around longer than you, that's why,' said my uncle and everyone gave little laughs.

That's something you grow to hate about adults: all the stupid laughing.

My aunt was wearing her silk dress and the long gloves which opened at the wrist so that the hand part of the glove could be folded back up the forearm. I thought they were stupid things.

We all had paper plates and the food was heaped into bowls in the centre. I liked the cold food. When my aunt came up, there were always plenty of good things to eat. This time there were little glass jars of chicken and prawns in a jelly she called aspic. There were lots of salad things like lettuce leaves holding hard-boiled eggs, grated cheese, grated carrot and sliced tomato and little bits of celery.

On the other plates there were heaps of sliced cold meats such as roast beef, corned beef and tongue, alongside mint jelly sauce and smaller dishes of mango chutney. I liked the chutney more than jam. Next to my uncle were a couple of kerosene tins full of ice and bottles of beer. We started in on the food and my aunt made sure I had plenty to eat. I spread the chutney on the bread and the surveyor's mate winked encouragement.

I wanted to talk, but I knew I shouldn't. So I sat listening as the surveyor and my uncle talked about the future of the farm and the fortune to be made from things like peanuts and dry rice in this new part of Australia.

'I was wondering about tobacco,' said my aunt with a smile. 'I'm sure we could organise a more modern processing plant. It's reasonably simple botanic chemistry, after all.'

'I didn't find any sort of chemistry all that easy,' laughed the surveyor. 'If it hadn't been for the war, I'd probably still be in Sydney trying to get through high school science.'

My aunt smiled again. 'I shouldn't be overly concerned,' she said. 'Australia is changing so rapidly, university qualifications hardly seem necessary to making money these days.' She was interrupted by my uncle filling beer glasses. 'Look at dear Ivan,' she said nodding at my uncle. 'He has one year of evening college in some sort of engineering something.'

'What about something for Jacky?' asked the mate quietly.

'Oh dear,' flustered my aunt and snatched up a few slices of buttered bread. She slapped on slices of cheese and one of roast beef. She put them on a plate with a sprinkle of grated carrot, a couple of radishes and handed it to me.

'Easy on,' warned my uncle. 'Probably his best feed this week.'

'Here you are, Mike darling,' said my aunt. 'Here's for your new friend.'

I hurried over to Charlie. He looked like he was nodding off to sleep, but he woke up as soon as I got there.

'Thanks, Boss,' he laughed, and took the plate. 'See if there's any chance of a mug of tea and a glass of water.'

'Certainly, Mr Rose,' I answered, and hurried back with his request.

My uncle leaned back and shouted that he'd get the primus going for tea as soon as he'd finished his fruit salad. Mr Rose waved by touching his forehead and one finger. It was like a salute and I tried to copy the action.

'It's the footwear I can't get over,' laughed my aunt quietly. 'I'm not sure if they're boots or the boxes they came in.'

Everyone laughed. It wasn't much of a joke, but I joined in.

'Where'd you get the boots, Charlie?' called my uncle.

Charlie tried to swallow, but couldn't. He almost choked on a piece of meat and had to pull it out of his mouth to answer. 'Brother-in-law,' he shouted back. 'Little sister married a yella fella down south. He still works with the air force and he sends us stuff from time to time. Good boots, Boss. Good boots for this country up here, hey.'

'Plurry good,' confirmed my uncle in a loud voice. 'You certainly got a good grip on Australia there.'

The others laughed. Except for the mate – he winced and looked away.

'He'll be the talk of the camp tonight,' said my aunt. 'Where'd you pick him up?'

'At the gate to the reserve. He was waiting there with half his tribe. All the lubras were there. He got in the back seat behind young Mick here.'

'Got a ride in the doctor's car,' laughed my aunt.

'They reckon that some of them earn a lot a loot up here,' said the surveyor's mate.

'You can say that again,' said my uncle. 'A plurry lot of money. They get about five quid a day picking peas in season, and they get about half that again cutting cane.'

'And they wouldn't spend much,' said my aunt. 'How much will you play Charlie for today?'

My uncle laughed and said something about that being a matter for boardroom negotiations. 'Besides, he hasn't got much to do. Young Mick does most of the hard yakka.'

I tried to protest, and told them about Charlie's blisters.

'Do him plurry good,' laughed my uncle. 'You keep your eye on him, Mick. Keep the old blighter up to the mark.'

'But he's a grown-up,' I said and blushed.

'Grown-up what?' asked my uncle.

I was lost for an answer, but the surveyor's mate started talking about buying a bit of land for himself with all the pay he got after being released from his POW camp.

'Must have almost made it all worthwhile,' said my uncle. 'I spent most of my war down in Brisbane. God, I tried to get away, but you know the army.'

'Yeah,' drawled the mate. I know the army. The Korean army, the Japanese army, the Australian army.'

My aunt brought the subject back to peanuts and tobacco, and soon after that the men finished their beers and we waited for the primus to boil the billy.

The afternoon wore on worse than the morning. The flats were dense with wild hops, each plant as thick as corn, but tougher. Charlie had to cut through the stalk and dig out a root to get a peg in.

In the middle of the afternoon, my aunt and uncle came round with a billy of tea and a few more sandwiches. My aunt brought me a couple of cakes as well. I offered one to Charlie, but he refused. All he wanted was to sit and drink his tea. His white beard had turned straw colour from sweat and he wiped his face on his shirt front.

The sun was going down when we finished. Everyone was tired out.

'Didn't want to come back tomorrow just to finish off,' said the surveyor.

'You might care to come over for a spot of dinner,' said my aunt. 'And if there is a Mrs Surveyor, perhaps you could bring her with you. Dinner will be very simple, I'm afraid. I'll have it brought up from the hotel.'

The surveyor said he'd like that, but all he longed for just then was a warm shower and a cake of disinfectant soap.

My aunt took the surveyor with all their gear in the boot. The mate took our ute. My uncle took the rest of the pegs in our car and I sat in the front seat, with Charlie kneeling up on the back seat, looking out the side window.

All the way, my uncle talked loudly about the season and said Charlie and his family could probably do all right putting in an acre or so of potatoes.

Charlie laughed and agreed with everything.

'You got boys, Charlie?' my uncle asked.

'Sure, Boss. Three big fellas and one sort of yella fella like your young fella here.'

'What age?' I asked.

'About fifteen, I reckon. Left school about a year ago now. You come over and he'll teach you fishing our way.'

'Does he use a spear?'

'No, Boss. Our way, not bush blackfella way. We use river net and line. All depends what you want.'

For the next few miles, we talked fishing.

We stopped at the reserve gate, not far from our own boundary, and Charlie climbed out. He was on my side of the car and waited for my uncle. He waited, smiling at me from time to time as my uncle rooted about in the glovebox for his wallet. By the time it was found and my uncle was standing in front of him, it was almost dark. The two of them were lit by the side glare of the headlights. Charlie's shirt and his hair looked sparkling white. His face was invisible.

'How much do you reckon, Charlie?'

'Okay, Boss, What you reckon, Boss? Hard work, Boss. Hard ground, blunt pegs, long day. Two days work in one, Boss.'

'But you got a ride in the big car, and your tea and tucker thrown in.'

'Sure, Boss. Good tucker that.'

'Well, what do you reckon?'

'Oh say a day and a half then. Should be four quid, let's say five quid, Boss.'

'But the boy helped.'

'Yeah, good boy that boy, Boss.'

'Well, let's say thirty bob, one and a half quid.'

'No, Boss. Not enough. Picking peas, I get four quid for smaller day.'

'All right then, Charlie. I'll chuck in another five bob and that's it. You got well looked after.'

Charlie looked down. I saw his shirt heave in a deep sigh.

'Okay, Boss. You're the boss.'

'Good man, Charlie,' said my uncle, and he handed over the money, adding the five shillings from change in his trouser pocket. 'There'll be more work soon. You stand by me now, I'll be able to help you and your family later on.'

I tried to call out goodbye, that I'd be over one day soon to learn fishing. But the words stuck in my throat. I tried to wave, but I saw Charlie's silvery head turn to look the other way as he slouched off into the dark.

My uncle climbed into the driving seat, opened his wallet again and flicked a five-pound note onto the seat beside me.

'Here's your share, Mick. That's for all your help.' He let the clutch out and we started down the track.

I picked up the fiver as though it couldn't be mine, not knowing what to do with it; knowing for the first time in my life, I was born on the wrong side.

First Trip

Queanbeyan

It was 1949, world peace was only four years old, and I stood, like the rest of Australia, on the threshold of a new life. I was thirteen and, for the twenty-third time in my life, we had moved house. I was happy about that. I was a couple of weeks into my sixth school and it meant life was back to normal! I knew the opening lines of introduction. 'Excuse me, sir. I'm a new boy.'

School was fine. Days went by of meeting new friends, learning new games. It was what you had to do in order to get a weekend to yourself that mattered. On the first two weekends, I had taken off, after breakfast, to walk the dirt roads, the cattle tracks and riverside paths and finally, I followed animal tracks through the scrub around Queanbeyan.

On the third Saturday, I met my first boss. I had spent the middle of the day sitting on the slip-rail fence watching my first sheep sale. Near the end of the sale, an explosive man who seemed to take the weather with him came into my life. He was a short round man wearing a pair of dusty army trousers, the usual elastic-sided boots and a khaki shirt. He started to move a pen of some twenty-odd sheep out of the sale yards and onto the road.

He saw me sitting there watching and in the loudest, clearest speaking voice I had ever heard he said, 'Here, son, help me draft out a few wethers, earn yourself a shilling.'

Draft wethers; I didn't have the vaguest idea what he meant. But I knew it meant a new bush start. We'd moved from Sydney. I was happy. So far, it wasn't up to Candelo, but at least it was country and there were no trams. All my time in Sydney I had longed to be back in the bush, daydreaming of breaking in brumbies, turning stampedes of cattle. All that.

My dad was still in the navy then and he'd been sent to the naval wireless station HMAS *Harman*. It was outside Canberra on the border with Queanbeyan. And there I was. Within two weeks, I was employed by a real-life stockman and we were going to become friends. I was going to make sure of that.

His name was Trotter and every afternoon after that I went to his little homestead called 'The Ranch' and helped him either yard sheep or clean out his horse yards. His wife was always happy to see me and one afternoon between them they ran in an old horse for me to learn on. Life began in earnest. There I was – a drover's mate. With my feet almost steady in the stirrups down each side of that quiet old horse, my new bush hat pulled down over my eyes and my whip held like a sceptre, I was mounted monarch of every paddock I surveyed. It's great to be in the saddle, in the bush you love with a passion – and you're nearly thirteen.

It was only a month after that, we set off on my first droving trip and we became a one-man, one-boy, two-horse, one-sulky and four-dog outfit. We packed our gear, slung a tuckerbox under the sulky seat, a bag of chaff for the horses on the floor; a horse rug over that; several hanks of rope along the sulky shafts; three dogs to run behind; and there between me and Mr Trotter sat Old Blue, the Queensland blue heeler. He was an ugly dog. He'd been in so many fights he didn't have a square inch of unscarred face. And he was savage. His main demand was space. We left at four in the morning and the moment we started up the track, Old Blue leaned over to me and with a soft, but menacing deep growl, followed by a show of powerful-looking teeth, told me to move over, that he needed space. My first reaction was not to surrender. My second reaction was to slink over as far as possible. I hated that dog.

The horses were more friendly. Socks pulled the sulky. Jimmy, the thoroughbred who'd won a race in Bungendore only a month before, trotted along behind the sulky. Mr Trotter drove the sulky and I held Jimmy's lead rein over the back. The other dogs ran along under the sulky and occasionally jumped up onto the tray to get a better view of the road.

To honour the event, I'd bought a pair of army disposal Light Horse leggings and the inevitable elastic-sided boots.

Mr Trotter had served in the Light Horse and he said something interesting about my leggings. Mr Trotter often said interesting things. He was a man possessed of a wondrous collection of oaths. I knew I couldn't use them for a few years, but I absorbed them all.

It was still dark when we started off. We trotted, jogged and walked through the dawn, into a sunny day till mid-day – then stopped for four hours. It had never occurred to me that drovers had extended lunches. We sprawled on the ground under a bit of a shady gum, ate our tucker and boiled the billy. Then, just when I wondered if we would ever move again, we harnessed up, rearranged our gear and set off down the road towards Yass.

Just on sundown, we got there. At least, we made the front gate just on sundown. A mile or so inside the gate, we trotted past the rabbiter's house, then another mile or so to the overseer's house, and then over a knob of a hill and down to the homestead.

The homestead was a mess of out buildings around a rambling, one-storey, colonial mansion. It had been built from the local blue granite. When we stopped, it was well into twilight. Alongside the house they had an enormous swimming pool; beyond that a cluster of outhouses, and down farther, two small horse yards and a wired-in poultry run.

We stopped by a side gate and the owner came out to look us over.

'You the drovers for tomorrow?' he shouted from the other side of the gate.

'Right on,' shouted Mr Trotter. 'We had a bit of trouble on the way. That's why we're late, mate. Everything all right your end?'

The owner growled back that everything with him was all right. 'We'll count out the cattle about half past seven in the morning. You blokes better doss down in the old laundry round there next to the butcher shop.'

'Thanks,' said Mr Trotter, one of the few times I ever heard him so gushing in his thanks.

We left Blue chained up under the sulky and went to inspect our sleeping quarters. The laundry was a large bare room with a cement floor, no washing tubs, but a wide open fireplace covered most of one wall. Mr Trotter sent me off to get an armload of wood and enough kindling to get the fire going.

As I left, Mr Trotter walked to the butcher's room next to us. He tried the padlock on the door. It was unfastened. 'We'd better lock that for him later on,' he said. 'All these crows about, anything could disappear.'

The wood heap was close to the homestead gate and the twilight was almost gone as I got there. And it was at that wood heap I had my first flight of road romance.

I walked around the great pyramid of cut wood which stood about fifteen feet high. On the other side, I met a girl. She was as tall as me with long dark hair, a simple wool dress and a little white apron; the idealised little woman of any young rouseabout. She saw me and smiled as if she was glad to see me. She gave me such a friendly warm smile, I fell instantly and hopelessly in love.

'Hello,' I stuttered. 'Do you work here?'

'Sort of,' she answered and she walked around the pile of wood and came right up to me. 'My daddy owns the station. What do you do?'

Somehow I managed to come out with what I had dreamed of saying for a few years. 'I'm a drover.'

'Do you like swimming?' she asked me.

I was about to answer, but at that very moment the station owner – the beautiful girl's horrible father – shouted at us from the veranda of the homestead.

'Helen! Come away out of that. Come here. Helen, come behind!'

The girl looked towards the voice.

'That your dad?' I asked.

'Yes. That's Daddy,' she answered. 'He's always like that.'

The shouting started again and she turned to go. But she spoke before she went. 'If you come again sometime, Mick, we'll have more time to talk.'

As she left, I picked up an armload of wood and scraped up a few handfuls of chips to get things going.

I had been gone no more than three or four minutes, but when I arrived back at the laundry, Mr Trotter had organised everything. He'd lit the hurricane lamp and, on the hob, waiting for the fire, were four lamb chops. The chops surprised me.

'I didn't see them before,' I said.

'I had them wrapped up,' he said and, 'You better keep your eyes open, Mickey boy. You'll see lots of things. Things you'll never bother to talk about. And here, use this dripping to get the fire really going.'

'Where'd the dripping come from?'

'Same place as the chops, I suppose. But I'll tell you this, mate. They didn't travel far.'

After that, I suppose I must have dozed off. But I was hardly asleep when Mr Trotter was shaking me awake.

'Come on, Mick, on your pins. Worko.'

I looked at my pocket watch on the cement floor beside me. 'But it's only half past three.'

'Not really. Time's different here. Anyway, what's five minutes here or there? Just now, pull your boots on without waking the dead. I've got a job for you.

The room was floodlit by an almost full moon. The fire was low and the air was freezing. I fumbled about for minutes before I could get my new elastic-sided boots on my cold feet. Mr Trotter pocked the fire to life and put on a few sticks of kindling. We both went outside and stood there listening.

'What's the matter?' I asked.

'Thought I heard a possum,' he answered as he folded an empty feed bag over his arm. 'But she's apples. Come on.'

We ghosted into a small yard. Not the big one with our own horses, but the station yard with a stable. A big grey stood asleep outside. Mr Trotter glided past him into the stable, found the feed bins and started ladling out dippers of oats into our empty bag.

'What you doing?' I whispered.

'Reckon we might feed the station horses. Sort of pay a bit of rent. And keep away from the doorway there, Mick. You might frighten the dogs.'

'But there's no need to feed their horses. The station hands do that.'

'Won't hurt to do a good turn, will it?'

But we didn't feed the station horses. Not even the big grey one. In fact, we carried the feed all the way back to our own horses and fed them.

'When'll we feed the others?'

'Actually, Mick, I just changed my mind. We may as well wait till morning.'

So we carried the rest of the oats, still the best part of half a bag, back with us to the laundry. But I wasn't so young as to swallow the story about feeding the station horses.

We rekindled the fire and at five I was sent down to collect (or steal, to be more accurate) a few eggs. Well, it didn't strike me as being a terrible act. Eggs are chicken feed in a way.

It was still dark. But the moon was high and it lit the ground frost like whitewash. A mouse could have been spotted at fifty yards.

The fowl house was a big open three-sided shed with a cement floor and a row of nest boxes along the far wall. The whole thing was safely enclosed by a high, wire-netting fence. Getting what I wanted looked easy. It wasn't. As I opened the wire gate and stepped into the shed, a nasty looking black 'n' tan sheep dog, chained to a nest, streaked out at me snarling and snapping. I stopped. What on earth to do? I had to get past him without being torn to pieces. Apart from that, if he started barking, I'd have to run for it and he'd have every dog on the place barking their heads off. I retreated a couple of steps to think the situation over.

I walked back to the sulky. Old Blue sat up snarling and sniffing the morning air. Gingerly I unfastened his chain at the far end and together we advanced on the fowl house.

The black 'n' tan saw me first. He lunged out ready to put on a show. And then he saw the difference and stopped in mid growl. Old Blue had made his presence felt. I let the old dog have a bit more chain. He took up the slack and suddenly I didn't hate him any more. He didn't bark. He didn't even show his wicked-looking teeth. His hackles raised the length of his back and he leaned on the air around that black 'n' tan. The sheep dog suddenly looked tram-sick. He shook his head, put on a bilious-looking grin and scratched his way back under the nest box until all I could see was a pair of almond eyes shining a silly looking welcome. I collected the eggs while Old Blue sat guard. Everything went to plan and Blue and I went back to the laundry together. That was when I discovered that, of the six eggs, four were made of china.

At half-past seven, the overseer arrived. By then, we had Socks and Jimmy rubbed down and harnessed. I was driving the sulky and I held Jimmy's reins over the back. Mr Trotter stood beside the newly mixed bag of feed. While I looked the other way, he asked the overseer to help him lift the bag onto the tray of the sulky.

'You always look after your horses like this?' the man asked, combing his fingers through the feed.

'Whenever I can, mate,' said Mr Trotter.

Old Blue simply moved over to make room.

By nine o'clock, we were away trotting, galloping, bellowing and fighting on the main road towards Canberra. It was misty and the cattle were nervous. Mr Trotter and the dogs propped and dashed from side to side to head off a bunch trying desperately to escape the mob and head back home. Mostly they were white-faced Herefords, but one small black bull at the back of the mob had to be watched.

All that time, I concentrated on Socks, the cattle in front, and keeping my eye on Mr Trotter. But there was something else I couldn't wait for forever. Gradually, but painfully, I couldn't ignore the memory of my grandma's advice as to what had to be done before you left home. I had not remembered her advice back at the laundry and I couldn't see how I could then solve the swelling problem out there on the road.

The mist was thick, the road behind me empty. It was too risky to climb down from the sulky. But somehow, no matter how many times I crossed my legs, my bladder, wherever it was, told me it had to be emptied. Mr Trotter was too busy with the dogs to look my way. I hoped the stinging pain would wear off. It didn't. It got worse. I had no choice. There was only one way. I turned and knelt up on the sulky seat facing the road behind me holding the reins over my shoulder and undid my army pants. It was difficult, undoing buttons in panic, arranging things and then – with shameful, but profound, if temporary relief – I started the process of urinating onto the road behind. I had just started when everything went wrong.

Out of the mist behind us came a car. It came slowly, a small black Hillman sedan, and it stopped just short of a stream of piddle. I tried to stop. It was impossible. I couldn't just finish piddling on the floor of the sulky. All that space was taken up with high-quality oats and our own tuckerbox. Nor could I stretch myself over the side. And it was all compounded by the fact that the four occupants of the car were Catholic nuns. They didn't laugh. They didn't even smile. Panic took over and I pushed the offending thing back inside my pants, still in full stream, and turned my back on the holy mothers. The driving nun blew the horn and came past me. They all looked at me, no doubt certain I was Protestant. It was hours before my pants were even a bit dry.

Mr Trotter got Blue to clear a lane for the car. He shouted for me to hold the cattle together at the back and ordered Blue to give me a hand. He switched sides and rode ahead along the left-hand fence, pushing the bullocks to the centre. He went out of sight and for some time I prayed that he would come back within an instant, if not sooner.

Blue and I pushed on for a couple of hundred yards until all became clear. Mr Trotter had turned the bullocks off the bitumen road and to the right – onto a travelling stock route. The new route was much wider and the bullocks settled down to walk and eat as they went. I was only sorry we hadn't turned off sooner. I would have been much more comfortable – and dry.

The mist cleared and we moved through a long patch of regrowth timber. The trees were close together and it made it hard to keep the mob together. They moved in many single-file groups, fighting among themselves to go either first or last when the going was tight. Mr Trotter kept them going, whistling the dogs to control stragglers. That was the first time I saw the young bull.

I knew he was young, if only because he had stumpy horns and he was shorter than all the bullocks. He made up for that in other ways. He'd worked his way back through the mob until he was right at the back with me and Old Blue. Not that he paid us much attention. He was determined to fight with a few bullocks and to ride an old cow. He was too short and she wouldn't stop walking. So he was restricted to rearing and trying to mount her whenever her tail was in his direction.

My own experience of mating was nil, but I wasn't impressed. For the cow, it was obvious that the Earth didn't move. For him it was not very satisfactory. He was just too short. The old cow was just unattainable. I suppose that was what made him angry. I made a mistake. I was annoyed with the bull, especially by his constantly trying to mount the old cow. I waved my whip at him and shouted. It was a silly mistake. We were in among trees, Blue was away somewhere and the bull heard me. He spun round and squared up to charge. There was open ground between us and there was nowhere on the other side for Socks to move. The little bull was about half a cricket pitch away when he lowered his head, bellowed in anger and charged.

I shouted for help. Socks pranced about on the spot in panic. I tried to turn him away so that the bull would ram the back of the sulky. I was again kneeling up on the seat and swinging the whip, but he kept coming. I saw Mr Trotter galloping over to help, but he wasn't going to make it.

But we did have help. I saw Old Blue behind the bull explode into action. He spun around and hit top speed in stride one. He reached the bull about five yards from me. The old dog clamped his jaws onto the fetlock of the bull. I could see the expression on the old dog's face as he clung on, being bounced and dragged along fighting like a thrashing machine. He was being thumped in all directions as the bull tried to kick and shake him off. But the dog clamped on. The bull bellowed in pain and tried to spin around and gore the dog. But Blue clamped tighter, all his strength flushing into his bone-crunching jaws. The bull didn't give up and twirled about, using his weight to try and free himself from pain. Mr Trotter roared in shouting and Jimmy rammed the bull side-on, knocking him sideways. Blue let go, Mr Trotter cracked his whip with a swirl of cracks. The bull limped for two strides or so and then charged ahead into the middle of the mob. The crisis was over.

We moved off again and slowly pushed the mob ahead. I moved Socks around in the open, keeping stragglers with the mob. It was time to daydream and to learn that there could never be another life like it. I would have to keep on going to school, but that was only part-time. My real job was being a drover.

Then we changed roles. Trott took over the sulky and legged me up onto Jimmy. I think Jimmy approved.

I tried to recite verses by Banjo Paterson. But somehow the dust, the heat and the millions of little black flies made Henry Lawson more genuine. I saw Hereford faces in the street.

We kept on well after sunset. We were breaking the law, but pushed on into the dark. The cattle were nervous and crowded together wary of passing shadows and the jingling gear. We had to keep going. We had no means to hold them together all night.

By about ten o'clock, we'd reached the abattoir home paddock, cut out the two extra into a small side paddock where they wouldn't be any bother and we trotted off back to the ranch. By midnight, I was home in bed. My first droving trip was over.

There were many more jobs. Some were longer, some shorter. It was a long time ago. But only recently, I received a letter with a newspaper cutting. It was news that Mr Trotter had retired. The local rag wrote of him, 'He's hung up his spurs for the last time.'

Certainly they'll sentimentalise about the passing of an era. They wrote that my friend Mr Trotter had gone to live in town. I'm sure he won't stay there long, and I wonder if he took the china eggs with him.

The Fox

Queanbeyan

He knew I was there all right. I think he must have seen the rifle. Not that that was something new to him. He'd been on the wrong end of a rifle on more than one occasion. In fact, to my knowledge alone, he'd seen the same rifle pointing at him on at least two occasions before that. But I was out to get him that morning. He'd been reported taking chooks and heaven only knows what else and, by way of back payment, was going to lose his life.

On that occasion, we came together in a small, rather open gully. I'd been lying flat on my face for a fairly long while, waiting for him to turn up. I knew he'd come along the creek; I'd seen his tracks on the mud several times. Then, just as I wanted to turn and scratch my knee or something, along he comes.

There was no rifle-clicking or cocking, but somehow that old fox knew. He slowed right down to a stop and then, very casually and defiantly if you like, he looked straight at me. He must have seen the side of my face around the tree. He didn't seem to bother much about the rifle, which was pointing at him almost point blank. He just stood off, like some superior being with a 'That's all for now, boy' sort of smirk. Yet he offered the sort of sitting shot a shooter doesn't really like. A point-blank, murder-in-cold-blood sort of shot. No escape for the fox, no chance of missing for the shooter. A shot that's a shame really.

That's what I thought as I squeezed the trigger. I'd aimed at a spot directly below the throat.

He dropped like a stone.

'Sorry, mate,' I said to myself, I was always rather sorry.

I stood up and walked towards him. As I did, I wondered if I'd take the brush – some kid might like it.

But the problem solved itself. I'd missed. Impossible! No one could miss. But I had.

I stood there absolutely bamboozled. It was ridiculous. The rifle was back leaning against the tree and I didn't even have a stone to throw. There was a blood trickle on the tip of his ear. It must have been because he rubbed it with his paw. He gave a slight wince. I was only about ten or so strides off him. His eyes flared up. I swear that old fox looked at me, not so much as if he was hurt, but just plain annoyed. With a savage look in my direction, he eased himself slowly to his four feet, turned around and trotted away in the direction he'd come from.

I didn't see him again for a couple of weeks. I'd heard reports of more hens being taken, but I never seemed to be able to get onto him. He'd changed his habits completely.

But later on I did see him one morning. It was fairly early while I was going around a few traps I'd set the night before. I had the rifle and threw a chance shot at him. He was loping easy on the hill. It was a long shot, but well worth taking. It was just a case of quick aim and fire.

The bullet must have just touched him on top of the hip. For a moment, his hind quarters sank to the ground. He sat snarling around him, but not for long. He stood up again and trotted away down the other side. I made up my mind there and then that I wouldn't shoot at that particular fox again unless I was certain I couldn't miss.

A few weeks later, I heard that some other dogman had had a shot at him, but missed badly.

The second-last time I saw him, I was riding home on a rough horse a young fella had just broken in for me. It was getting on for dark and I'd had a good day – four foxes in the afternoon, so I was happy about things. I saw him coming up from the river by a fair-sized red gum. There used to be a lot of them. I recognised him at once, and I suppose he might have recognised me.

He was jogging along in such a way that, if he kept going the way he was, we would cross halfway up the short hill. He didn't change his direction and, as we came together, he broke into a lope and bounded across in front of the horse. I couldn't have got the rifle out of the bucket anyway, but I wanted to have a look at the fox close handy, if I could. And then blow me down if he didn't turn and run beside the horse like a flamin' sheep dog. He wasn't more than six or eight feet away. I could see the chip knocked off his ear and the nasty scar on his rump where I'd taken the potshot. Suddenly I felt a bit of affection for the old creature.

'Why don't you buzz off home!' I yelled down to him.

The horse shied a bit, the old fox turned a disdainful look up at me and jogged off at an angle, over the hill.

That was about two years ago. Of course, the last time I saw him was only about two weeks ago. Next week, I retire. So I don't suppose I'll see him again.

What with the bad season this year, following the more or less good one we had last year, there's plenty of stock and animal life around. But it's in pretty poor condition. I was riding down into what we call Softwater Gully. It's fairly steep-sided, pretty thickly wattled, and has a decent sort of flat along the dry creek. Years ago they used to grow a bit of lucerne there.

As I was picking my way down, the same old fox jumped out from behind a box tree. He must have been sleeping, I think. Anyway, I drew a bead on him and just as I was about to fire he stopped dead and turned around.

I watched him this time. I fired. He seemed to drop a split second before the rifle went off. But it was too late to aim again. It was a bit too uncanny somehow. You'd swear he could see me thinking. And he didn't seem to drop naturally. It was more like something else. As if the ground itself pulled him down to it. The earth clung to that mangy old fox like it loved him. But I meant to have a second shot just the same. By aiming at the ground underneath him, I reckoned he should cop it sooner or later.

I cocked the rifle again and was just aiming, when a shadow circled around the flat. I looked up. It was a wedge-tail eagle – probably a young'un. 'Wonder what she wants,' I said to myself. Anyway, I didn't watch her for long.

I looked at the old fox again. He was just making off, giving me the sort of shot I wanted. A running three-quarter, side-on shot. But before I could even squeeze the trigger, it happened. The eagle hurtled out of the sky and crashed onto his back.

For a second or so, what with those giant flapping wings and what I suppose was the fox rolling around, I couldn't see who was getting what. I'd never seen an eagle go for fox before. If I'd thought in time, I might have got the both of them with one bullet. There used to be a bounty on wedgies. But nature doesn't cooperate like that for very long. The next moment, the eagle hopped free and hovered a yard or so over his head.

He stood his ground taking in the situation. I suppose it was new for him as well. To escape from me, he had to make a run for it. To escape from the eagle, he had to stand and fight. Once on the run, the eagle would get him, but if he stood still, he must have known I'd have him. He'd already lost the rest of his wounded ear and there was blood on his shoulder. But he hadn't given in.

He made a quick glance, first at me, then at the eagle. Then suddenly he sprang forward. It was only a short spring, but enough to put a clump of timber between himself and my rifle. At the same time – thinking I suppose, he was making a bolt for it – the eagle flew at his neck. I suppose I was easy fifty yards away and I could hear the thumps and snarls from where I stood. Not that I stood for long. I'd dismounted and moved myself into a ringside possie about fifteen feet away.

First, the two of them stood off, watching each other. The wedgie was weaving her neck from side to side trying to distract the fox, to make him move into an awkward position. Her wings were half-spread to balance and she moved lightly from foot to foot. The old fox, he stood pat in a sort of low-hunched set. His jaws kept open at the ready and his tail stuck up in the air like an angry cat's. Everything about him was tense but calm. Nothing moved except his eyes.

I moved closer to get a better view still. They seemed to stand looking at each other there for hours, the one weaving about trying to catch the other off guard, the other steady, waiting for the first to make a mistake. Suddenly the eagle lost her patience. She let out a shriek and jumped at the fox's head. She'd made a mistake. She couldn't even land well. Her talons clawed at nothing. The moment she was in the air, the old fox dropped, rolling his forequarters and landing on one shoulder. The wedgie had to land on his ribs. She dug those talons right into his bones. Not that it did her much good. With a quick lift, the old fox rolled over, pinning those talons under his body.

The noise for the next few seconds was terrific. It was a mixture of high-pitched panic shrieks and the throaty-menace growl of the fox. Then just as suddenly it all stopped. The fox must have got the eagle by the neck. She lay on the ground a fluttering heap of feathers.

He stood in the same spot, He was scratched and bleeding all over and I expected to see him drop dead as well.

But he didn't. So I lifted the rifle and aimed. He looked up. He saw me all right. He must have known that I wouldn't shoot him then. He looked at me. And as casual as you like, he started licking his paws, right under the muzzle of the rifle.

I put it down and grinned. 'Hardly worth it for a few bob.'

He stood up and jogged across the flat and into cover in the rocks.

That was two weeks ago. I won't bother to go after that old fighter again. There's a lot of weekend shooters around the place nowadays. One Saturday, some bloke will come up from the city and shoot that old fox. The skin won't be worth too much, but I suppose he might earn himself some sort of local reputation.

I'll be sorry when that old fox gets killed.

The Long Jump

He lay his paw on the surface of the water like a cat about to step on glass. The pressure was so light, the surface of the water stretched down before his pad went through and into the creek. His foot was moved with such deliberate delay it seemed the entire night would pass before the water touched his shin. A few fleas casually avoided the rising water as if they'd done it all before.

He heard the jangle of bit and harness as the stockman forced his horse to lurch awkwardly down the bank a bit farther away. He listened for the two sheep dogs. He stood, slowly sinking farther into the creek. His first paw touched gravel bottom as the dogs started to lap at the crossing. He repeated the action with his second foreleg and stood for a moment in an awkward position with his tail higher than his head.

His movements were imperceptibly slow, almost an exercise in control. The fleas scampered in massed groups onto his back toward the safety of his neck as his haunches sunk deeper into the water. The brush tail submerged and the fleas moved in droves along his back toward his shoulders. Gradually, he allowed his haunches to move down, sensing and controlling the speed of the sinking.

The horseman ducked his head to avoid the willows and stopped the horse at the edge of the creek.

One of the dogs snarled, knowing a fox to be present, but uncertain where. They were footsore from working and they lay their bellies in the water as they drank.

The stock horse shook the bridle, rattling the bit between his teeth, and snorted at the shadows. Like the dogs, the horse knew he was there, somewhere in the shadows. The horse had known, in fact, on at least two previous occasions. But the stockman was tired. He thumped his heels into the horse's ribs and the four of them went splashing through the shallows. They walked up the hill towards the farmhouse, the rickety poultry yards and the stinking hollow-log kennels.

The fox concentrated all his senses – disturbed. Usually, there were two horsemen. The one who had just crossed through and another one, similar, but smaller, the one who sometimes sang as he rode, who rode faster, who had hunted him once on a horse and he'd had to criss-cross through barbed-wire fences to get away.

His haunches touched the floor of the creek and he switched his tail from side to side. As the horseman went into the darkness on the far side, fleas hurried up the back of the fox in what soon became mass panic. He sank into the water follicle by follicle.

There was nothing in his world just then, save his concentration on slowly sinking. But this was sharply shattered with a triple roar, whine and echo. A gun barked on the hillside behind him.

He froze and waited. He knew he was not connected with the sound. He had heard it in the past many times. Sometimes, there had been a connection between himself and the sound. Once with his mother, the gun had barked and his mother had died. There had seemed then no connection between the two things, the barking and the death. There had seemed to have been no responsibility from the gun. Only the obvious fact that something linked the two happenings. The gun barked on the hillside again. He listened, but sank lower into the water. By the time he gun barked the third time, only his head was above water.

The third bark came and was sickeningly different. He himself was untouched, but in that instant of its barking, he knew he had somehow been deeply and irreparably injured. He twitched his ears in rejection.

Gradually, his neck and ears went down till only his muzzle and ears remained above the waterline. He concentrated his vision on the fleas overcrowding on the bridge of his snout. He lifted his muzzle slowly and the fleas fled to the highest point. He could almost focus his sight on the end of his nose. Then followed his first rapid movement.

With a shake, he submerged his entire head for a fraction of a second. His head lifted and shook again. He subsided once more with the waterline below his muzzle and eyes. There were only a few fleas left. Once more he submerged. When he surfaced, all the fleas had gone.

He stood in the water listening. His work was over for the moment. He knew that somehow he had been viciously if remotely hurt, and he moved out of the water to stand in the shadow to drain.

He paused and moved off at a steady trot, his head low and his tail balancing his stride. His night had been fractured by the barking of the gun, so instead of moving towards the poultry sheds, to the hole he'd found in the fence the night before, he moved back towards the far hill, to his earth with his vixen and her four cubs.

He went first by the side of the creek. As he jumped the big log, he disturbed two rats. They panicked and headed for the trees across open ground. Before they could reach the first tree, he had overtaken both. He killed the first by simply snapping his back with a single bite, and he dashed on to overtake and kill the second. He hurriedly ate both, crushing their bones before he swallowed. He loped off around the base of the hill and up to the gum trees and into the scrub of wattles with the large burrow he had made to his earth.

The moment he reached the mouth of the earth, he understood. He had vaguely understood while he had been in the creek, drowning the fleas. But it was in the moment he reached the mouth of the earth he understood that the bark of the gun had killed his vixen.

The four little cubs came falling over each other's fat bodies to reach him. They still smelled of their mother's milk and they had been waiting for her. He rolled them about his snout, playing them into a state of tired fun. When they were tired, he regurgitated the two half-digested rats onto the floor of the earth and watched the cubs eat.

He knew that like his father, he would have to rear the cubs himself. He breathed in the smell of the vixen in the earth. The homesick scent of her was strong. The cubs smelt of her and he wanted her alive in the earth.

The cubs ate and rolled together to sleep. He went to the mouth of the earth and looked at the curdle of cold stars. Slowly, spite filled him, his tail stiffened erect behind him like a young pine tree, and, with the start of a plan, he set off stiffly, back along the creek. He went through the water above the ford, downwind of the poultry yards, and loped up the hill in a state of controlled anger.

He took the hole in the fence in his stride and dived through the small hatchway into the poultry house. He was inside and below the perches before a single fowl knew of his presence. They slept above him, fat, their crops flowing over the perches, their feathers cuddling their feet.

He sprang at the first one and had her down and dead before she made a sound. He sprang at the next and she landed with a squawk. He snapped her neck and then snapped the next. There were loud panic cackles from several hens at once. One hen saw him and dropped to the ground in fright. She lost her head for the trouble and he jumped around the shed like an over-sprung, repeating jack-in-the-box, teeth snapping and cracking at every lunge. The live hens flew against the wire netting as he snapped and ripped them. He tasted hot blood in his throat, felt the burning sensation in his eyes, snapped with hate, and broke bones with pleasure.

He would have killed the lot, but for the arrival of the station's big red dog. The dog smashed through the hatchway like a crazed bullock. He barked, bashed and bounded about, blinded by feathers and flapping hens. He barked again and tried to crash into the fox in the dark. The fox went under his nose and out the hatchway.

Other chained-up dogs outside barked in chorus and the big dog crashed out after him. The fox ran twice around the lemon tree in the yard to give the dog time to catch up. The dog was only a short distance behind him, barking uselessly and smashing the countryside as he ran.

The dogs urged him on. From the far side of the poultry yards, a man was shouting. The fox darted through the hole in the fence. It almost broke the dog's neck. He couldn't fit and turned to run up and down the wire, trying to find another hole. The fox sat outside watching and waiting.

The dog, in desperation, returned to the small hole and, with a screaming, wire-tearing effort, squeezed and crashed his way through. He lumbered after the fox, who sat waiting his time before turning to run towards the creek.

The fox had time on the other side of the creek to sit again and watch the dog splash-jumping through the water like a pair of horses.

He longed to kill the dog, but there was no possibility of such a thing. In a close fight, the dog would clumsily tear his smaller body to pieces.

The dog came through the water, shook himself and followed the fox up the hill. The fox had been there the night before. He had carried a hen up the hill and buried her for a rainy day. He went past the spot and saw the two legs still thrusting up from the soil. But the soil now stank of man. He knew it was now a place that could not be trusted and that man had done something to the ground. The hen's legs weren't as they had been the night before.

He sped away curious and angry. He was tired of the big dog, he wanted his vixen. It was then he heard the bark of the gun again. There was no death or hurt, but he knew that this time, there was a connection with himself and he wanted to be away and rid of both the dog and the barking gun.

Again the gun barked and he felt wind fly past his body. The dog came charging behind and he heard a man ahead shouting the dog's man-given name.

The fox sensed instant panic, realising he was running towards the barking gun. If he turned back, there was the strong possibility of the dog catching him before he reached the creek. In a hard straight run, he knew the dog could overhaul him.

The gun barked yet again and he felt a stinging on the top of his right ear. He felt that a small part of his ear had gone with the bark of the gun. He slowed momentarily, and the dog almost caught him by the tail.

In that moment, he planned.

The fox collected himself, jumped and somersaulted up and backwards, passing over the dog before the big creature registered what had happened. He slowed his run for the dog to wheel around and follow. He let the dog come within biting distance. His tail trailed behind like an invitation.

The dog snapped but missed. The fox saw the legs of the hen thrusting up from the dirt in front of him. He headed straight for them. The dog snapped at him from behind as he steadied to jump.

As he reached the edge of the new soil, he again collected and stretched into the longest, gliding jump he had ever made in all his nights of hunting. He skimmed the legs of the hen in mid-stride.

As he landed, metallic snapping and bone-crunching sounds behind were over-screamed by dog cries of agony.

The fox landed on firm ground and ran on for a few strides before stopping. He spun round, sat on his haunches and carefully groomed his right forepaw as he watched the writhing agonies of the dog.

Man had buried a circle of rabbit traps around the dead hen and the dog had been caught. At first, it was only one leg, but as he thrashed about trying to wrench free, two more legs were snapped and broken in the steel jaws. The big dog flopped about whining and crooning in a delirium of agony.

The fox sat for a moment, then lay in the grass to roll, lost in the pure joy of the exquisite pleasure of revenge.

The dog continued to whine and whimper for mercy. The fox licked his paws once more then turned and trotted off across the face of the hillside. He wouldn't come back this way for a long time. There was now the smell of man and the even worse smell of dog.

As he trotted along easily, the gun behind him barked again and the dog noises stopped. The fox thought with some concern for the cubs rolled up together in the earth, and he broke into a long smooth well-balanced lope. Tonight they would have chicken, but from the next farm.

Preludio

Galicia, Spain, 1976

My grandma never saw Spain. But for all that, she never lost her abiding hatred for General Franco and all he stood for. She was an avid reader of Spanish history. She loved the various forms of Spanish music and she knew of a Spanish poet called Lorca.

As a boy, I absorbed the same hatred and over the next thirty-odd years I learned nothing to ease that revulsion.

So in 1978 I was in the north of Spain. On a much-postponed honeymoon with Luisa, the Spanish girl I had met in London eighteen years before, and with whom I had corresponded through thirteen intertwining years across ten Third-World countries and who I finally joined up with again in Kavieng and married in Port Moresby in 1976. The wedding took place not long after the death of Franco.

I was happy to be on holiday with Luisa in Burgos among her parents and family and we had gone to Asturias to meet a family of cousins headed by David and Tina. They had already been told, or warned, that I was a Celt of Irish descent. On that account, they wanted to show me anthropological sites from which the Spain-domiciled Celts had migrated en masse from Asturias and Galicia to the then empty land of Ireland.

And there was a special site they wanted me to see – the caves of Altamira, famous throughout the world to everyone but me. I knew there were special caves in France with walls decorated by cave artists, but I didn't know of such places in Spain.

Luisa quietly filled me in on the history of the caves, that they were decorated some twenty thousand years before the Christian era; and that my lovely cousins, by marriage, were sure I would marvel at the drawings I was about to see. I was happy to agree. In fact, I was happy to agree to anything that would please them all.

By that year, I was reasonably fluent in Spanish after having worked for the UNO in five Latin American republics, and could join in on most conversations.

We arrived in David's car at the opening of the caves and waited for our guide to arrive. It was the off season and tourists were not encouraged. Flashlight cameras were a no-no and the professional guides were all away that day at a seminar.

After half an hour or so, our stand-in guide arrived. Throughout the year, the man was a shepherd taking his flock of sheep and goats in great arcs around the mountains. That da,y he had offered to be our guide. He was proud of both his jobs – especially that of a volunteer cave guide as it had been a shepherd, like himself, who had discovered the inside caves. Legend has it that that earlier shepherd had chased a wanton goat to the very back of the cave and found a tunnel along with a heap of ancient artefacts such as spearheads and stone axes. Eventually he had slithered on his belly into the tunnel. It was impossible to turn around, so he followed it through into a vast unknown cave of wet floors and dripping stalactites. It was pitch black. Even the tunnel allowed no light to enter and he made several forays with a lantern before he understood what he had found.

Our guide arrived with his official lantern and asked us not to take photographs or to shine any torches, as our lights would damage the paintings. He explained that since that first discovery, anthropologists had opened the cave by drilling a door through the rock wall where we waited. He opened the iron door, switched on his pale lantern and we entered the world of 20,000BC Spain. At first, I could see nothing, even with the help of his torch. The darkness clammed around me like a blanket. Luisa and her family stood close to me to ensure I understood everything the man said. The shepherd explained the age of the cave and how the cave people of that far-off time had accepted the cave as a sacred site. It was obvious that he also believed, to his very keep, that the cave was sacred. For him, it was a cathedral.

Gradually, my eyes adjusted to the dark and the shepherd's torch lit paintings of bison, deer, elephants, hunting parties of men and women, of cooking fires, spears and animals long extinct. I was amazed by the pictures, by the way the artists had taken the rock face as part of the animal's body. The colours and highlights of the animals, the bright eyes of the hunted bison reflected the pale lamp light as if they had been drawn there the day before. He went on to explain how more and more pictures were being slowly uncovered, that the wet walls over the millennia drip down a thin skin of limestone over the pictures. He went on and gradually I began to sense something else, to feel apart from it all.

I was back in Candelo drifting off into the house of oranges in the horse paddock. I suppose I stopped listening. Luisa sensed that I had drifted off and quietly, and politely, told me in English that I should listen, that it had all been arranged specially for me because I was Celtic. I tried to listen again, but couldn't. I felt a gnawing need to turn away and peer up into the darkness. David and Tina also sensed my looking away and asked Luisa if something was wrong. Luisa quietly, though no longer so politely, ordered me to pay attention. But I couldn't. I wanted to, but couldn't. The shepherd tried to pretend that I was listening. But he couldn't go on. He stopped talking and looked down. Then he beamed his lamp in my face and asked me in Spanish if something was wrong. I assured him I was more than happy, that nothing was wrong.

He tried to go on again and I tried not to keep turning away and looking up and away into the dark. He gave up, paused a moment and asked me nervously if I was looking for something different. He had a strange tinge of fear in his voice. I tried to say no, but it was useless.

Luisa and her cousins were whispering together nervously.

I heard Tina say, 'What's wrong with him?'

I felt ashamed, but I didn't know what was wrong with me.

The shepherd reached out, gently held me by the forearm and quietly asked me, 'What are you looking for?'

'I don't know,' I said stupidly. 'I'm sorry, but there's this feeling there's something special up there.'

'What do you think it is – this something special?'

It was too late to lie. 'I think it's a small horse.'

The others gasped. They were whispering the word horse among themselves, no doubt wondering if the Irish are given to moments of madness.

'What sort of horse?' he asked and I felt a stronger edge of fear in his voice. His face was close to mine and he looked at me as if imploring something.

'I don't know what sort of horse,' I said. 'I'm sorry, but I just feel that I have to look up there behind me in the dark.' I pointed up into the pitch dark.

The shepherd sucked air through his teeth and increased his grip on my arm. The others were silent.

'Look,' he said, and he turned his lamp in the direction of where I had pointed. 'Look,' he said nervously.

I watched his pale light move across the high wall at the back of the cave. Then we all gasped. Up there, in a clearing of flat stone, was a painting of a small, but fat white horse. His mane stood out in a tangle and his head was half-turned to look down at us. I started to shiver. I tried to control everything about me and tried to talk.

'It's so high,' I said. 'Why on earth would someone have put that little horse up there by himself? Who would have done such a thing – and how?' Immediately I knew it was a nervous and silly thing to say.

The shepherd gently squeezed my arm. It was more like a caress and he spoke directly to me – quietly as if speaking to someone from another time. 'Perhaps it was you.' he said quietly.

After that, we didn't stay much longer. We came out into the light and the shepherd embraced me and kissed me goodbye. I sensed he was off to tell his wife and friends about the strange Irishman and his horse.

From then on, we had a wonderful day. We saw abandoned Celtic villages with their roads and stock yards. We saw crematoria and the ruins of meeting halls. I was amazed by it all, but throughout that day the little horse stayed with me, trotted around me in everything I said and did. The little horse has never really gone away and it took me another five years before I could sit down and write the story of how he came to be up there.

Antlers

20,000 BC

A few nights ago when I was lighting my reeds, my mother's mother told me that one of her old aunties remembers the time when we didn't have fire at all. In those olden days, there was no cooking, no dancing at night, no stories to look at in the fires. We'd never have had all the fun we had yesterday – well, last night anyway.

It all started yesterday morning, out there in the front cave with my sister. She was laughing as she ran from the cave and I wanted to chase her; catch her before she reached the clearing and there, with an elaborate ceremony, pretend to kill her with a make-believe, short spear. Of course, she would keep on laughing, she's always laughing. But she'd play the game and lie down and kick about like a wounded she-wolf.

I jumped to follow, but stopped. Uncle shouted after me from down cave and I looked back to see the chisp of light which meant he'd lit the reeds and was about to enter the tunnel.

'Antlers bring more reeds,' he called out in his friendly voice.

It was him who gave me that name. He called me Antlers because my hair stands out around my head instead of falling down like my sister's. This uncle is the one who teaches me things. Last summer, he taught me hunting with the spear; how to kill the boar on full charge.

I like his lessons out there in the laughing sunshine. But it isn't the same inside. In there, in the crying night, far into the deep cave beyond the tunnel, there is no light, no heat, no trees, no grass; nothing but them. They are demons no one has ever seen. But you know they're there; you feel them all around you, all the time.

The day before yesterday must have been their day for hunting. They were there all the time that day. I stood in there watching uncle working at his bison, colouring in the red body, putting black for the legs and the horns. Later, he used the same black for the spears and the hunters in the distance. But even though I stood as close as I could, so that the burning reeds could warm me, one demon swept down from the dark and got behind me. You can't see them. But what happens is that one of them will come like a cold skin and suddenly flatten onto you from behind. It makes your whole body jump and your teeth start rattling; and while your teeth are rattling, another one will get into your body through your nose or mouth, or under your arms, and they put fright into your every limb. Sometimes they make you run like a mad thing. Other times, you are so full of them you can't move and you just fall down, shaking on the spot.

The day before yesterday, it was like that. One got onto me from behind. I started to wobble, but I managed to jump in the dark and I jumped over the fire. That's the best way. The demons can't beat fire. They can't jump through the fire like we can. Well, they can, but they don't come out the other side like we do. But that day, I wasn't so lucky, because when I jumped, another one was waiting for me on the other side, and uncle spun away from his work, caught me up in arms to protect me and put me in a big bearskin he keeps for the deep cave. After that, he threw pieces of fire into the dark to keep the demons well away. But fires out there in that all-time night don't last. I tried to keep the bearskin tight around me. But they only need a chink uncovered and in they go. Well, when uncle saw that I was being attacked without any let-up, he sent me outside to work with my sister.

That night around the cooking fire, he told my mother that I was brave under attack. But he also said he would take me again into the deep cave and one day soon, I would start my own picture; that he would find a special wall for me and prepare fire reeds that would last a whole picture.

'Antlers,' he called again. But this time his voice was sharpened with that flinty sound. He was impatient. He stood at the mouth of the tunnel holding the reeds and his colours under his arm.

I watched and I could see how he lay down on his back to scramble through the tunnel, into the darkness. Uncle always wants me to follow – to go with him into the deep cave. He knows that although I am always being attacked by the demons, and although I don't like the dark, I am always happy to see his magic pictures.

Inside the deep cave, between the place where uncle works on his bison and the opening from the tunnel, somebody's great-uncle, or great-great-uncle has already painted a bison. It is near the bottom of the wall and now it is being slowly covered again by the dripping stone. Uncle says that another wall was once completely covered with bison and other strange animals. But the dripping stone lays down a skin on top to keep them safe. The cave is like that. It gives you lots of lessons. It does things slowly, but always in its own way. It it weren't for the demons and the dark, I would be happy to stay in there all day.

'Antlers,' my uncle called again through the tunnel. His voice from the night had a big sound and suddenly brought on the shudder demons, as if part of them still stayed deep inside me.

I started to shake and immediately I jumped and ran for the sun, straight down the ravine path and knowing my sister was only a little way ahead. But she is fast, my sister, when she likes. She is probably the fastest runner in the cave. No one has a sister who can beat her.

She was running steady as I came up with her, as if waiting for me. Her long skinny legs stretched out in those long low lopes of hers. She had told me one night, as we lay wrapped in our big deer skins near the story fires, that she once saw deer running on level ground. They hadn't seen her, so they were not frightened and they ran as she did, In fact, she told me, she learned to run like that just by watching the deer. Nowadays, other girls watch her, trying to learn her ways. But when they do it, they only look a bit like her. When she runs, she doesn't look like herself, but like a deer; that's the difference.

She was running to reach our special tree, on our side of the great ravine, to see the uncles come through. I would stay with her this time, perhaps for the last time. Soon I would have to join the uncles in the big party.

'You won't go back inside with uncle?' she asked without even puffing.

'I'll go tomorrow,' I said. 'Or if I have time, I'll go later on, before night.'

She laughed her own little laugh. That means she understands more than what is said. She knows a lot, my sister. She is older than I am and she's the one who teaches me things inside the front cave.

I've got lots of sisters and I don't know how many brothers. Some have already gone with the good demons like my great-uncles. There are many more brothers and sisters of other aunties in the cave. But this sister is special. She understands me and about my being frightened of the deep cave.

She told me only the night before that if she were an uncle, or even a boy, she would never ever enter the deep cave, but would work in the sunshine with the deer and the bison. She said she knows of one uncle who, even though he is an old man, has never been brave enough to enter the deep cave through the tunnel. He lays down bits and pieces or food, or old spearheads near the opening instead.

When she told me, I wondered if it would be possible for me to do the same. But then, I have been inside. Not just once, but many times. I have wriggled through that tunnel into that great everlasting crying night. I have fought with them. I have jumped through fire to burn them off. No one could say I have tried to buy them off. Besides, old spearheads wouldn't do; they know rubbish when they see it. Demons aren't stupid.

The day was starting to dry away the mist. And above us the side of the mountain had a rock face turning from grey to yellow in the morning sunshine. We loped together down through the cork trees and passed the big boulder where uncle and I had killed our first big boar last hunting.

The ravine is where we trap deer and sometimes even bison. It is a small round mountain with a great open split down through the middle. They say that one day in the olden times, one of the old gods lost his temper and, with his bare hand, he chopped down on the mountain and with one hit he split the mountain from top to bottom. You can do it yourself. But first you have to make a little mountain out of mud.

On our side of the ravine, the mountain is thick with cork trees. They grow right to the edge of the cliff. The gap between the two sides is only as wide as a good deer jump – and on the other side there are no trees for as far as a good spear throw.

Three aunties were out collecting wood for the cooking fires and they waved as we went. In the next clearing, our Magic-man was making spells with mushrooms. He was too busy to look up and we circled out as far as possible.

We stopped at our special tree near the edge of the ravine and the moment we stopped, we heard all the shouting over on the other side.

My sister said she heard her favourite uncle, but she couldn't hear exactly what he shouted. 'He's just making noises, I think,' she said, laughing again.

We all like him. He is always laughing, like my sister, and at night he tells magic stories to block the forest demons from sliding into the cave. They're not so bad as the deep-cave demons and they only come in to get warm, but you don't want that sort of thing snooping about the cave at night when you're trying to sleep.

'In the olden days,' my sister whispered to me as we sat on our special branch, 'there were many caves with many more people and they would make big fires to scare the deer over the cliff. But these days, the old ways are being forgotten.'

She looked thoughtful for a few moments and I wished I had been born older. You'd know more.

From our branch, we could look down and see the bottom of the ravine. There were ten or more uncles standing about among the rocks and talking. Most of them had axes and some had tree clubs.

Across on the clear side of the mountain, nothing moved. But we could hear the uncles among the bushes beyond the clearing shouting louder and louder as they danced closer.

We sat waiting and my sister told me again a story about the time when a special boat came up along the edge of the land with sails made from something like thin skins. The people in the boat gave miracle things in return for wolfskins and a few lumps of heavy yellow rock. She told me in a whisper of how the stranger people did bad things with some of the people in the cave and so our then Magic-man, the great-great-uncle of our present Magic-man, made a monstrous wind to come. The wind lifted their boat up out of the water and flung it and smashed it against the sea rocks. Most of the strangers were drowned. Those who didn't drown were killed in the water by our uncles. She said it would have been against the rules to let them come out of the water alive.

'What happened to the miracle things?'

'No one really knows,' she said, watching the ravine. 'They were put in a secret place by our old Magic-man and no one knows where that secret place is.'

'One day I'll find it,' I said quietly.

'Then we'll have all the miracle things,' she said, and we sat talking about what we'd do if we all the things from the secret place.

While we were talking, I pulled a leaf and started to nibble.

'That leaf has rivers inside it,' she said.

'Where?' I didn't really believe her.

'Look,' she said, and snatched the left from me. She avoided the wet part where I'd had it in my mouth and she held it up against the sun and there, sure enough, were lines running everywhere through the leaf. See what I mean about older people knowing things.

I had a good look at the leaf after that and I quietly promised that if she taught me many more things, I'd give at least half the miracle things to her when I found them. She smiled and said something about having heard such talk before. That's the only thing I don't like about growing up. The bigger you get, the less you believe in things; especially promises.

I might have sat there thinking about promises and things for a long time, but there was movement on the far side. It was just the bushes at first. My sister clutched my arm in case I might get too excited and fall. There was a swell of shouting and the uncles on the bottom of the ravine started shouting up as well. Then there was a flurry of confused movement behind the bushes and just after that I saw the first deer.

He was the biggest bull deer I'd ever seen and he carried a rack of antlers on his head bigger than all his body. It was enough for heaps of knives and plenty of diggers. But he carried the rack like it was just so many feathers.

He danced out shyly into the centre of the clearing, looking about him everywhere. Then just as fast, he sprang back behind the bushes. Then he was out again, then back again. The uncles were still somewhere behind the trees shouting and making magic noises. The big deer trotted back more nervously this time and brought five or six females. Just then, more deer tiptoed out to get close to the others, some of them with little ones jumping about the clearing trying to hide underneath their mothers.

'They are frightened,' laughed my sister. 'They think the forest demons might get them.'

I laughed. I told you my sister knows lots of important things.

Then many more deer came out, till there were twenty or more, and they tried to keep away from all the noise. When they heard shouting from the bottom of the ravine, they tried to run back again. Next they tried to run down the side of the ravine. But aunties were hiding among the rocks on both sides and they came out shouting and waving sticks.

When the deer saw the aunties, they tried again for the trees. But they couldn't because of all the uncles. Only the deep ravine yawned open in front of them.

The deer families started running about, jumping and leaping like mad fish in the river. Soon all the uncles were out of the trees. They walked in a line spreading their sticks and spears. They shouted like thunder spirits and danced magic steps to stop the deer getting through between them. The noise was frightening, not only for the deer, and I took a good grip on my sister's arm, just in case.

The big deer trotted to the lip of the cliff and sniffed. He shook his antlers in anger at the ravine, stabbing and rattling the air about him. He stopped, collected himself and the next instant, bounded straight for the gap. He sprang from the lip and arched over to land on our side.

He propped, turned and called to the others. They trotted about near the edge, but were too frightened to jump. So he trotted off half a spear throw, turned and rejumped the gap to land back with all the others. In the air, he left a bridge behind him like a rainbow. The dancing uncles closed in behind, and the aunties moved up from the sides. Suddenly, the big deer with the antlers galloped his family in a circle, almost touching the uncles as if trying to find a way through the spears and the killing sticks. But there was no gap and he wheeled the family again and galloped for the lip.

As the big deer turned, I felt a strange new sensation. It was as if someone had tried to touch me on the shoulder to make me turn and make me look behind. But I didn't and the big deer of the antlers took his whole family head-on for the gap. He was at top speed as he jumped and only a few strides in front of the others. He was well in the air when the first of the others started their jumps. He landed on the far side and let them pass.

The first six or more landed on our side and I heard angry shouts against the deer-protecting demons from all our uncles below. But again I felt the touch to turn and look behind. But I knew there was nothing there except the mountain.

I watched the gap and again I saw the big deer recross his rainbow to the rest of his family. Again I felt the urge to turn, to make me look back over my shoulder, and almost without knowing why, I did. This time, there was not just the mountain. Up high, there was a strange clearing. The mist and the cloud had opened just enough to let a shower of sunshine pour down and drench that clearing.

When you see things that look normal, but you know they are not, you get a little jump inside. Your neck does tight and you cover your mouth with your hand so that demons can't get in.

Up there in the centre of the clearing, as if there just for me, stood a small white horse. He stood fat and solid, his head high, looking across the mountains to the sea. The sunshine lit him so that his white coat tinged yellow. The rest of the light bounced off and sparkled all about him in the air like sunshine on the spray around a waterfall.

In that instant, I knew it was a vision. In the next breath, the horse turned and beckoned down to me with a toss of his head. And then, just as suddenly, my vision disappeared. The sun pulled back its pouring and a cloud closed over. My horse was gone. But the picture of him stayed in my head. Somehow he was more than just a horse. The memory of him called on me to act.

Visions are like that; they make you do something. It's just that I had no idea what I had to do. But all of me, inside me, called me to do something; to mark down forever that visions can happen to ordinary people like me. I looked back at the ravine and watched the deer. But inside me, I saw only my horse on the mountain. I wanted to tell my sister, but I listened to my insides and my insides said I mustn't – not yet.

The big deer faced the gap with his family and he bounded yet again with the others close behind. The uncles ran forward shouting because the deer were jumping and landing safe on our side.

Then, just in time, our own demons started working. A big doe missed the gap. Her forelegs scratched at the far cliff trying to pull it close for some invisible footing. She spun in the air and fell, going slowly at first, twisting and tumbling end over end, her tail and legs flaying about, kicking and writhing till she walloped-stop on the rocks below.

Four or five fawns also tried to jump. But they were too small and they couldn't hold their footing on our side and followed the doe down forever.

I saw, with half my looking, the uncles below, running about killing those deer who tried to flop about on broken legs. The big deer of the antlers took the rest of his family into the safety of the forest. I was happy to see him escape.

My sister scrambled down and ran to join the uncles and the aunties in the ravine. I saw her go and heard her call me. But in my insides, I still only saw my vision of my horse and I knew in my most secret, most inside places, that the horse had somehow for some strange reason, picked me out and touched me.

I stumbled down into the ravine and helped cut up the deer with the new knife uncle had chipped for me. I talked to the uncles and aunties around me, helped another uncle cut up a fawn, and finally I helped an old auntie carry half a deer back to the cave. But my thoughts were up there in the clearing behind me.

As soon as I entered the cave with auntie and put the deer near the cooking fire, two great-aunties came to help and they sent me off to be with my sister. They are usually good like that. I've got one great-auntie who's my mother's mother. She's the one who really looks after me. So I started to walk from the cave, when suddenly I felt two things happen at the same moment. When that happens, you always have to do a third thing. I was struck inside me by my vision of the horse, and outside me, on my skin, I felt a longing for cold. The two things somehow meant something as if there were magic in the mixing. So I let something happen. I stood still and, sure enough, I felt a good demon enter my body through the nose. It made me breathe in deep and I filled with him. The more I sniffed, the more he entered, and after that I knew I couldn't be in any danger. With the good demon inside me, a bad demon outside can't get in. There just isn't any room.

I let the good demon take over the secrets in me and lead me about. Demons, even good ones, can't talk. But they know how to lead you about from your insides. If one wants you to collect an antler pick and you try to pick up fire sticks instead, the sticks will seem heavy or thorny and you'll drop them. Then you will pick up the antler pick almost without knowing. Sometimes you have to pick up many things before you really know what it is he really wants.

But this time it was easy. The cold, the wanting to feel cold all over, took me towards the tunnel of the deep cave. There were a few things lying there, an old spearhead and a few spear stones probably left by our frightened uncle. I bent down and took one up, but it was not right. So I dropped it. Besides, it was junk.

There were many bundles of reeds at the opening and I picked two. They came up easy. So it was right for me to pick them up. The good demon helped in that. I knelt and looked into the tunnel. There was nothing in there but the great elemental fur of black. But now, it was a long-haired, soft, furry black and, while it cooled the outside of me, it warmed me inside.

So I lay back on the ground in the entrance to the tunnel for about half a spear throw, holding the reeds in the dry. Not that I could see them. Once you are in the night, inside the tunnel without lighted reeds, you can't see your hand, even if you touch it on your nose.

It was a long time in the tunnel, but you know when the tunnel is ended because suddenly there is not so much fur around you, and you know you are in the big opening of the deep cave. The blackness gets thinner. And it's wet in there, with water dripping and making tree trunks of stone up from the floor and even down from the roof. I stood up and peered over to the left. There in the distance I saw the tiny light from uncle's reeds. I called to him that I had brought more reeds for his light. It wasn't the real reason I came, but that's what I said. You have to say something.

Uncle was finishing the black legs and horns of the bison and he'd put in a few more hunters and lots of aunties. As soon as I saw the bison, I looked down and saw a big deer drawn there by someone else's great-uncle. The deer was falling near the bottom of the wall and in that moment, I saw that it must have been our same ravine with a falling deer and uncles below with killing sticks. Even the aunties being put there by my uncle were in the right place and for just then – I was again with my sister on the branch of our special cork tree.

I stood with my eyes closed and I saw the ravine on the wall, the deer below. Then I heard uncle singing life into his own bison so that he would look happy and bring other bison. I heard him singing, 'Breath of my breath which is the breath of the Good Breath within me. Fill you and keep you safe forever more.'

I stood with the one bundle of reeds still under my arm and felt again the pull to turn and peer behind me. This time I followed. As I turned, I leaned down and lit the reeds. The fires spluttered to life and spat at the dark with sparks of light. I studied the light for a moment and then slowly turned as the good demon wished. Above and behind me opened the great black of the cave, I held the light in front and saw nothing. So I stepped forward and held the light away behind me, looking up as I had looked up from the cork tree.

I laughed in the dark. Because, up there as if shining in the swallowing blackness, was a clearing. The light from the reeds touched it, high at the back of the cave, high among the crying trunks of stone trees. Without saying anything, I lit more reeds and collected my colours from the spare skin bag that uncle keeps for me. When I crouched down, a bad demon tried to wrap me, but I coughed with contempt at his silly effort. I was too safe for the worst of them. For all I cared, they could all come and try, none of them could touch me. I still had my vision; I was still filled with the good demon. For as long as I stayed awake, nothing could touch me, or destroy me,

I walked into the deep of the dark. Uncle called after me, something about being careful. I told him over my shoulder I was with a good demon and I went, leaving him singing to his bison at the ravine.

I was about half of half a day finding a way to the clearing and it was climbing and slipping all the way. Many times, I thought the good demon had left me and once the bad demons almost killed my light.

They lured me under a dripping stone and some of my reeds lost their fire. But the others stayed lit and, although I scratched myself badly on dripping stone trees, I arrived at the clearing.

It was a plain, dry wall about two uncles high and three or four sleeping in line. In front was a good shelf of dry stone for me to work from. I opened the bag and I allowed my hand to take the colour black. Then without any help at all, my arm floated up and started to draw with strong, quick lines on the white stone wall. In no time at all, the little horse stood in the clearing as if alive. As if he had always lived there. Within a quarter of a day of drawing and colouring, my vision was there forever.

If you go there now, even if you need someone else for a guide, you will know how he really came to stand up there; up there alone in his own clearing.

I put more lines away from him in red to hold off the spears of sunshine and I put other secret lines to keep away any bad demons that might grow jealous. And all that time of drawing, the good demon in me sang and I felt my face warm and my spirit bubbling through my insides. So I stood there a while, lost in the moment with my horse, and I leaned in close to his face and breathed into him, 'Breath of my breath which is the breath of the Good Breath within me, fill you and keep you safe forever more.'

I sang it again and again, till I felt it fill him completely. Then as if the good demon inside me said I was too close, I stepped back.

It is always a silly thing to do. You never walk backwards in the night. I could have backed over a cliff. Instead, I stumbled against something different. I knew I had stumbled against something like basket. At first I was just pleased it wasn't a cliff or a monster. Then as if the thought had been hanging around inside me trying to get out, I wondered how anything like a basket could be up there behind me in the cave.

I spun around with the reeds and there it was. It was a basket all right; but not our style of basket. Ours are rough and fat like cooking pots, but this one was flat with a basket lid. Ours never have such things, though my sister had told me one night that long ago a ship came up the coast and the people there had baskets of many different sorts, even baskets for holding fish. I tried to lift one end and the good demon didn't stop me. It was heavy, but I could manage.

As I edged down from the clearing with the basket, I looked up and in the dancing reed's light, flickering among the stone trees, the horse's head nodded up and down as though to say, 'Now you know why I brought you.' And his nod said I could return whenever I needed to talk of special things; that he would wait for me, or you if you like, up there in the forever night of the dripping stone forest.

Uncle was nervous at first. He thought there might be bad magic in the basket. He had never seen such a basket, though he too had heard the talk about boat people who used such things.

He waved his burning reeds all around the basket just in case there might be some bad demon sitting on it. 'Better to be sure than sorry,' he said. Then he shook it. There was something inside all right.

So while I held the reeds close, he lifted the lid with his stone knife and held it just a little way open. We waited in case something bad wafted out. There was a new strange smell, but nothing else wafted out. Nothing heavy floated out and we felt safer.

Uncle lifted the lid and it yawned right open and lay quiet as if glad its long-held secrets must be kept no longer. A skin, but not a skin, lifted out easily on the knife and uncle held it. It was as big as a skin for winter, but it wasn't skin. It was light and folded about any way at all. In the light of the reeds, we could see it was the yellow of morning on rocks.

The new cloak skin fascinated uncle, but I saw in one corner something shining like a dog's eye at night. I snatched it up and it came free. But not by itself. It was on a string. I turned it this way and that in my fingers and sometimes it would light out with a red light of its own. It was hard like rock but smooth chipped like a flint knife. But this stone had a life of its own, some gentle, red-shining demon locked inside.

I knotted the string and pushed the red stone into my colours bag while uncle pushed the new skin into his own bag. Then — without saying much, we started to move the basket towards the tunnel and the cave.

At first, there were only a few aunties cutting up deer and they were afraid to come near us. One of them ran, calling to the people outside. Soon others came and one went back for our Magic-man. He came angry and unsteady, waving his magic stick, so most kept more than arms left. He also brought his bag of colours and before stepping over the basket, he marked magic signs on his face and chest. Some of the people started wailing when they saw the signs; as though he had opened up old worries. Then with his magic stick and his arms outstretched, he advanced on the basket.

Our Magic-man heard the story through from uncle nodding to make him hurry. He listened, but kept his eyes on the basket. In fact, on a strange thing like a round flat stone. It was yellow and on the face of it was a face like a man's face. The Magic-man kept his magic eye on that little yellow face all the time he listened.

When uncle finished telling about my little horse, the Magic-man started to sing a quiet magic. Then he walked three times around the basket and tapped it seven times with his magic stick. Following that, he muttered things to the basket in an old language that none of us could understand.

'All this now belongs to us,' he said after his long singing.

Everyone moved forward a step or two as if to see what bit belonged to each of them.

The Magic-man stopped them. 'This has been returned to us through a vision,' he said, and there was a murmur among the aunties and I felt warm inside.

My sister moved next to me. I could smell the cooking fire on her body. She had taken off her top skin and her body was soft and slippery from all the cooking.

'This is our group reward because we have a boy among us – Antlers

– who is not afraid to follow the bidding of the good demons. Let it be a lesson to many of you, who think only of yourselves,' he said.

Old uncles were nodding and felt the Magic-man was not really praising me, but warning the others. But I liked it just the same.

'These are the miracle things from the bad boat men of long ago,' he said.

The uncles and aunties grunted in surprise and looked at the Magic-man, who knew everything.

The Magic-man kept his eyes on the little yellow face. 'There is to be no fighting, or the deer will go and the rain will never stop. The children will rise against the uncles and my magic will put pain in the ears and teeth of the wicket.'

People pulled their skins around them as if cold. But really they were frightened sick.

'There is a special power in the basket. It must not be touched by anyone save me.' He then looked at the roof of the cave, waved his magic stick and roared like an angry bison.

People shrank back a little, but not so far as to miss their chance when he gave permission to help themselves.

The Magic-man bent down and snatched up the yellow face. He held it up for all to see and many were afraid of it. 'It can see inside the thinking of every man and auntie at every moment,' he warned.

The Magic-man stopped scowling and carefully tied the yellow face to his neck string. It lay back flat against his painted chest and he flung his arms wide, turning to beam the new little face on all.

Then he stepped back. 'The miracle things are now returned to us. Care for them,' he said, and walked out of the cave towards his magic clearing and his magic mushrooms.

At first, the people were afraid to move. But suddenly, as if all decided together, they rushed the basket.

The basket was already decaying and broke under so many hands and feet. Inside was one skin bag full of strange things. Things like stone knives made from red metal, smooth and sharp. There were many of them and of many sizes. There were many more skin things, but they tore apart when many people tried to keep the same piece. There were small baskets of stone on strings and wolves cut from yellow stone.

One skin bag held a small yellow man who had two faces, one for each side of his head. An auntie said we should put it near the front of the cave because it looked both ways at once and would warn us of attack. Everyone agreed and she went off to put it high on the rock ledge at the mouth of the cave. It's still there.

Everyone played with the new things till eating time. At eating, we had cooked deer and two uncles told stories from out wonderful past. Then three of the aunties danced to show how they had skinned the fallen deer.

I was falling asleep as I watched, so I went off to find my sister and we snuggled into our bearskin to sleep. She was happy with me and promised to teach me even more running. I tried to stay awake to listen and I heard her saying that now that I was someone special in the cave, I would soon have my own skin bed to sleep among the uncles.

It was then I remembered and pulled my colours bag into the skins and took out the red stone. Even in the light from the story fire, the stone lit red. I had not shown it to anyone and her eyes opened up as if not believing such a thing could ever exist.

'What will you do with such a demon?'

'I will keep my promise of the cork tree.'

'How?'

I felt the good demon in me float out my hand to her, felt her take the stone from me, sensed her putting it around her neck under the skins, sensed the warming feeling she had for me rush out of her towards me. I lay there warm inside and comfortable.

She kept on patting my head and telling me of all the ways she would teach me to run so that I could outrun any wolf in all the forest. She quietly went on and on. I felt her breath on my face as she sang me to sleep.

'Breath of my breath which is the breath of the Good Breath within me, fill you and keep you safe forever more.'

I liked that. And I heard her sing it for the second time as I slowly slipped among the gentle demons of sleep. As I passed on the way down, I saw again my little horse. He stood alone and unafraid, high up in the forever-dark of the cave's dripping stone trees; master of his own clearing, a sign for anyone who feels the touch, and can't help turning.